The King's Justice

The King's Justice

Stephen R. Donaldson

GOLLANCZ

LONDON

Copyright © Stephen R. Donaldson 2016
All rights reserved

The right of Stephen R. Donaldson to be identified as the author
of this work has been asserted by him in accordance with
the Copyright, Designs and Patents Act 1988.

First published in Great Britain in 2016 by Gollancz
An imprint of the Orion Publishing Group
Carmelite House, 50 Victoria Embankment, London EC4Y 0DZ
An Hachette UK Company

A CIP catalogue record for this book is available
from the British Library

ISBN 978 1 473 21449 1 (Cased)

1 3 5 7 9 10 8 6 4 2

Printed in Great Britain by CPI Group (UK) Ltd, Croydon, CR0 4YY

www.stephenrdonaldson.com
www.orionbooks.co.uk
www.gollancz.co.uk

The King's Justice

he man rides his horse along the old road through the forest in a rain as heavy as a damask curtain—a rain that makes dusk of midafternoon. The downpour, windless, strikes him from the long slash of open sky that the road cuts through the trees. It makes a sound like a waterfall among the leaves and branches, a damp roar that deafens him to the slap of his mount's hooves. Ahead it blinds him to the road's future. But he is not concerned. He knows where he is going. The broad brim of his leather hat and the oiled canvas of his cloak spare him from the worst of the wet, and in any case he has ridden in more frightening weather, less natural elements. His purpose is clear.

Shrouded by the deluge and covered by his dark gear, he looks as black as the coming night—a look that suits him, though he does not think about such things. Having come so far on this journey, and on many others, he hardly thinks at all as he rides. Brigands are no threat to him, even cutthroats desperate enough to hunt in this rain. Only his destination matters, but even that does not require thought. It will not until he reaches it.

Still his look does suit him. *Black* is the only name to which he answers. Many years ago, in a distant region of the kingdom, he had a name. His few comrades from that time—all dead now—knew him as Coriolus Blackened. But he has left that name behind, along with other pieces of who he once was. Now he is simply Black. Even his title rarely intrudes on who he has become, though it defines him.

He and his drenched horse are on this road because it leads to a town—so he has been told—called Settle's Crossways. But he would have taken the same road for the same purpose without knowing the name of the place. If Settle's Crossways had been a village, or a hamlet, or even a solitary inn rather than a town, he would still have ridden toward it, though it lies deep in the forests that form the northern border of the kingdom. He can smell what he seeks from any distance. Also the town is a place where roads and intentions come together. Such things are enough to set and keep him on his mount despite the pounding rain and the gloom under the trees.

He is Black. Long ago, he made himself, or was shaped, into a man who belongs in darkness. Now no night scares him, and no nightmare. Only his purpose has that power. He pursues it so that one day it will lose its sting.

A vain hope, as he knows well. But that, too, does not occupy his thoughts. That, too, he will not think about until he reaches his destination. And when he does think about it, he will ignore himself. His purpose does not care that he wants it to end.

The road has been long to his horse, though not to Black, who does not protract it with worry or grief. He is patient. He knows that the road will end, as all roads must. Destinations have that effect. They rule journeys in much the same way that they rule him. He will arrive when he arrives. That is enough.

Eventually the rain begins to dwindle, withdrawing its curtains. Now he can see that the forest on both sides has also begun to pull back. Here trees have been cut for their wood, and also to clear land for fields. This does not surprise him, though he does not expect a town named Settle's Crossways to be a farming community. People want open spaces, and prosperous people want wider vistas than the kingdom's poor do.

The prosperous, Black has observed, also attend more to religion. Though they know their gods do not answer prayer, they give honor because they hope that worship will foster their prosperity. In contrast, the poor have neither time nor energy to spare for gods that pay no heed. The poor are not inclined to worship. They are consumed by their privations.

This Black does think about. He distrusts religions and worship. Unanswered prayers breed dissatisfaction, even among those who have no obvious cause to resent their lives. In turn, their dissatisfactions encourage men and women who yearn to be shaped in the image of their preferred god. Such folk confuse and complicate Black's purpose.

So he watches more closely as his horse trudges between fields toward the outbuildings of the town. The rain has become a light drizzle, allowing him to see farther. Though dusk is falling instead of rain, he is able to make out the ponderous cone of a solitary mountain, nameless to him, that stands above the horizon of trees in the east. From the mountain's throat arises a distinct fume that holds its shape in the still air until it is obscured by the darkening sky. Without wind, he cannot smell the fume, but he has no reason to think that its odor pertains to the scent which guides him here. His purpose draws him to people, not to details of terrain. People take actions, some of which he opposes. Like rivers and forests, mountains do not.

Still he regards the peak until the town draws his attention by beginning to light its lamps—candles and lanterns in the windows of dwellings, larger lanterns welcoming folk to the entrances of shops, stables, taverns, inns. Also there are oil-fed lamps at intervals along his road where it becomes a street. This tells Black that Settle's Crossways is indeed prosperous. Its stables, chandlers, milliners, feed lots, and general stores continue to invite custom as dusk deepens. Its life is not overburdened by destitution.

Prosperous, Black observes, and recently wary. The town is neither walled nor gated, as it would be if it were accustomed to defend itself. But among the outbuildings stands a guardhouse, and he sees three men on duty, one walking back and forth across the street, one watching at the open door of the guardhouse, one visible through a window. Their presence tells

Black that Settle's Crossways is now anxious despite its habit of welcome.

Seeing him, the two guards outside summon the third, then position themselves to block the road. When the three are ready, they show their weapons, a short sword gleaming with newness in the lamplight, a crossbow obtained in trade from a kingdom far to the west, and a sturdy pitchfork with honed tines. The guards watch Black suspiciously as he approaches, but their suspicion is only in part because he is a stranger who comes at dusk. They are also suspicious of themselves because they are unfamiliar with the use of weapons. Two are tradesmen, one a farmer, and their task sits uncomfortably on their shoulders.

As he nears them, Black slows his horse's plod. Before he is challenged, he dismounts. Sure of his beast, he drops the reins and walks toward the guards, a relaxed amble that threatens no one. He is thinking now, but his thoughts are hidden by the still-dripping brim of his hat and the darkness of his eyes.

"Hold a moment, stranger," says the tradesman with the sword. He speaks without committing himself to friendliness or animosity. "We are cautious with men we do not know."

He has it in mind to suggest that the stranger find refuge in the forest for the night. He wants the man who looks like a shadow of himself to leave the town alone until he can be seen by clear daylight. But Black speaks first.

"At a crossroads?" he inquires. His voice is rusty with disuse, but it does not imply iron. It suggests silk. "A prosperous cross-roads, where caravans and wagons from distant places must be common? Surely strangers pass this way often. Why have you become cautious?"

As he speaks, Black rubs casually at his left forearm with two fingers.

For reasons that the tradesman cannot name, he lowers his sword. He finds himself looking at his companions for guidance. But they are awkward in their unaccustomed role. They shift their feet and do not prompt their spokesman.

Black sees this. He waits.

After a moment, the sworded guard rallies. "We have a need for the King's Justice," he explains, troubled by the sensation that this is not what he had intended to say, "but it is slow in coming. Until it comes, we must be wary."

Then the farmer says, "The King's Justice is always slow." He is angry at the necessity of his post. "What is the use of it, when it comes too late?"

More smoothly now, Black admits, "I know what you mean. I have often felt the same myself." Glancing at each of the guards in turn, he asks, "What do you require to grant passage? I crave a flagon of ale, a hot meal, and a comfortable bed. I will offer whatever reassurance you seek."

The farmer's anger carries him. Thinking himself cunning, he demands, "Where are you from, stranger?"

"From?" muses Black. "Many places, all distant." The truth will not serve his purpose. "But most recently?" He names the last village through which he passed.

The farmer pursues his challenge, squinting to disguise his cleverness. "Will they vouch for you there?"

Black smiles, which does not comfort the guards. "I am not forgotten easily."

Still the farmer asks, "And how many days have you ridden to reach us?" He knows the distance.

Black does not. He counts destinations, not days in the saddle. Yet he says without hesitation, "Seven."

The farmer feels that he is pouncing. "You are slow, stranger. It is a journey of five days at most. Less in friendly weather."

Rubbing at his forearm again, Black indicates his mount with a nod. The animal slumps where it stands, legs splayed with weariness. "You see my horse. I do not spur it. It is too old for speed."

The farmer frowns. The stranger's answer perplexes him, though he does not know why. Last year, he made the same journey in five days easily himself, and he does not own a horse. Yet he feels a desire to accept what he hears.

For the first time, the tradesman with the crossbow speaks. "That is clear enough," he tells his comrades. "He was not here. We watch for a bloody ruffian, a vile cutthroat, not a well-spoken man on an old horse."

The other guards scowl. They do not know why their companion speaks as he does. He does not know himself. But they find no fault with his words.

When the sworded man's thoughts clear, he declares, "Then tell us your name, stranger, and be welcome."

"I am called Black," Black replies with the ease of long experience. "It is the only name I have."

Still confused, the guards ponder a moment longer. Then the farmer and the man with the crossbow stand aside. Reclaiming the reins of his horse, Black swings himself into the saddle. As he rides past the guards, he touches the brim of his hat in a salute to the man with the sword.

By his standards, he enters Settle's Crossways without difficulty.

In his nose is the scent of an obscene murder.

⁓

He finds the town much as he expects it. The street is dirt that has been scattered with gravel to provide purchase for the wheels of wagons, and also to give some protection from mud for the townspeople. But the day's heavy rain has overwhelmed the gravel. The street resembles a quagmire, and the alleys between the buildings are worse. Fortunately for the pedestrians, every place of business on both sides has a wide, raised wooden porch sheltered by a slanting roof. The folk of Settle's Crossways can move between taverns and general stores, milliners and inns, with little exposure to the downpour's aftermath.

Or they can pass between places of business and houses of worship. Some distance ahead, Black sees the crossroads that brings trade and travel from every point of the compass to and through the town. That intersection is a large open square. And opposite each other on its corners, northeast and southwest, are temples. Both are made of framed timbers, both have porched entrances with high doors, both thrust bell towers heavenward. There the similarity ends. The intended white dazzle of the Temple of Bright Eternal has been much raddled by the rain, while the black walls of the Temple of Dark Enduring glisten even at dusk as though they have gained an obscure victory.

Bright Eternal and Dark Enduring are the gods of the kingdom, worshipped as such, bombarded with pleas and praises. Yet their hymns sound much the same, and their liturgies vary little. In truth, they have too recently acquired their stature as gods for their modes of worship to become distinct. Also Black knows that they are not gods. He is more familiar with them than any inhabitant of Settle's Crossways, priest or parishioner. They are elemental energies, nothing more—and nothing less.

He is a veteran of what he calls the Balance Wars, the conflict of shapers hungry for power. That contest cost the lives of all his former comrades. More often than Black chooses to remember, it came close to killing him. Indeed, it would have reduced the known world to rubble if the King, a shaper himself, had not forsaken warfare to become a focus of balance, the human mediator between the unknowing, unthinking, and uncaring forces of bright and dark.

For good reason, Black distrusts temples. He fears that a preference for one god or the other will encourage the ambitions of shapers. In themselves, bright and dark are not fearsome. They are merely necessary. They are, after all, the elemental energies that enable the world—life and death, growth and decay—when they are balanced against each other. The danger is that taking strength from one makes the other comparatively stronger. Then the balance tilts. And it is imbalance that generates true power, the power of shapers to remake themselves and their allies and their desires.

Without the King—

Black does not think about such things. He knows too well what they entail. He does not wish to recall old horrors. The reek of a present atrocity is more than enough to resurrect wrath and fear from their graves deep in his soul.

The folk of Settle's Crossways want the King's Justice. No doubt they have tried to summon it. No doubt their congregations pray for it daily. But they do not know what it means. They have no idea what the King's Justice is.

When Black has secured a stable for his mount, he makes his way along the porches to the nearest tavern. It stands conveniently near the crossroads and the temples. The townspeople he passes stare at him, or make studious efforts not to stare. He has that effect, but he does not ignore it, despite its familiarity. He touches the brim of his hat to everyone, a greeting to assure men, women, and children that he is harmless.

Between him and the tavern, a mother and her young daughter approach. They have come from a milliner and are walking homeward. To them, also, Black touches his hat. But when he has passed them, the girl says, "Ma, that man has holes."

She is too young to understand caution.

Black halts as though a hand has been placed on his shoulder. While the mother tells her daughter, "Hush, child. Be polite. He is a stranger," Black turns to look more closely at the girl.

"But Ma," she insists. "He has holes in his *soul*."

The woman takes her daughter's hand, intending to urge the girl away. But she pauses when Black lowers himself to one knee in front of the child. Surprised, the mother stands still.

Black studies the girl, a child of no more than five or six years. She is clean and well-dressed, from a comfortable family, but he ignores such details. He ignores her blond ringlets and her open face and her unbruised knees. Instead he concentrates on the fact that she is not afraid. He concentrates on the kindness in her eyes. It suggests concern for him.

"Holes?" he asks gently. "In my soul?"

He knows too well that the girl is right. He has spent pieces of himself in more battles than he cares to remember.

The mother is anxious now. "Forgive her, sir," she says. "She will learn courtesy when she is older."

At the same time, the girl says, "I see them." She points at his chest. "They are there and there"—she points repeatedly—"and there and there."

Still gently, Black says, "You surprise me, child. There are few who see me. Even fewer see me clearly."

His manner encourages boldness. "Ma can't see what I see," she proclaims. "She thinks I make it up. But it is all true.

"Your holes hurt you. If they get bigger, you will die."

———

Black frowns, considering her words. After a moment, he admits, "That is certainly true."

The girl extends her hand. She means to touch him. "I can make them go away." Then she becomes less sure of herself. "They are too big. I can make one of them go away. When I am older, I can do more."

Before her hand reaches him, Black rises to his feet. Now he faces the mother, who is beginning to pull on her daughter's arm. "You are wise, madam," he tells her with less of gentleness, more of warning. "You have a gifted child. A precious child. You do well to protect her. She will have time enough for her gifts when she is a woman."

He knows now that this child *can* heal him. But he also knows that doing so will blight her childhood. She is a seer, one who sees. True seers are more rare than shapers. They do not cause imbalance. Rather they draw strength from within themselves. The girl is indeed precious. But she is too young to suffer the cost of what she can see and do.

The mother feels sudden tears in her eyes. She has been troubled for her daughter, disturbed by a child who pretends to see things which do not exist. But the stranger believes that such sight is not a pretense. This both comforts and frightens the woman. She casts one more glance at the man to confirm that he is serious. Then she hurries her daughter away.

Black *is* serious. However, he does not consider the child's presence dangerous, except to herself. Certainly he craves her healing. He aches for it when she is gone. Yet her gift has no bearing on his purpose. Her scent is as clean as her person. He does not regret sparing her.

Touching his hat to all who pass by, he continues toward the tavern.

Like the town itself, the tavern is much as he expects it to be. It has a wooden floor strewn with sawdust, a long bar with ale-taps along its inner edge and shelves of bottles and flasks behind it, a number of round tables with chairs for four or six, and an increasing count of patrons, some of whom have settled themselves for a night of drink. All this is indistinguishable from other taverns around the kingdom. The only differences here are the general affluence of the patrons, the consequent comeliness of the barmaids, and the room's air of unresolved distress. These men and their few women take comfort in drink rather than in each other. Comradeship, jests, roistering, and songs do not numb their fears.

Many of them look at Black as he enters, and of those many stare. But he touches his hat to them and leaves them alone. He already knows that the cause of the town's alarm is not present. If it were, he would smell it.

Its absence, also, he does not regret. He is patient. And he has been taught by blood and pain that no good comes of confronting his foes before he has prepared himself.

To begin his preparations, he seats himself at the bar one stool away from a man who is already dedicated to drowning his concerns in ale. Black does not remove his cloak, though his arms are covered by the heavy sleeves of his calfskin shirt. His hat he wears to cover the scars on his scalp. From the barkeep, a large man too well fed and lubricated by his own wares to contain his sweat, Black requests ale. He asks a bowl of stew, and bread with it. And when his desires are met, he concentrates on eating and drinking like a man who has no other purpose, though in truth he does not relish the stew, and the pungent ale does not ease his mind.

The barkeep's name is Bailey. His nature is friendly, but the town's alarm makes him wary. Also he is both interested in and suspicious of the stranger. He hovers nearby while Black eats and drinks.

After a time, Black asks with an air of indifference, "You are not troubled by brigands?" He knows this by the lack of walls and gates, and by the inexperience of the guards. "I am surprised. The forest can hide any number of evil men, and your crossroads surely offers many opportunities for plunder." He appears to address the barkeep, but in truth he is speaking to the drinker near him. "How does it happen that you are spared?"

"Trouble we had, sir," Bailey answers in his most pleasant tone. "In my Da's time, that was. Lives and goods were lost, fearsome quantities. My Da kept an axe here, under the bar, to defend himself. But the old wars have been good for us. Caravans now come with squadrons of men-at-arms, and even lone wagons are guarded by archers and pikes. No brigands trouble us now. They attack only in the deep forest, where they can be sure of escape."

Black is doubtful, but he puts the matter aside for a later time.

"You are fortunate, then," he observes. "Other regions of the kingdom are not so blessed."

"We are, sir," Bailey replies. "We are." He means to say, *We were*, but caution stops him. He knows, as all the town now knows, that strangers must be distrusted. Striving for still greater pleasantness, he asks, "You know the kingdom, then, sir? You are much traveled?"

Black has not met the barkeep's gaze. He does not now. "Much traveled," he assents, "yes." Then he deflects Bailey's prying. "Enough to observe that in favorable times the Temple of Bright Eternal attracts many good folk. It is Dark Enduring that responds to woe and hardship. Is his Temple well attended?"

He believes it is. The Temple of Dark Enduring is as large and well-maintained as its neighbor.

Bailey thinks to offer some dismissive response, but politely, pleasantly. Before he can choose his words, however, the man seated one stool away mutters with his mouth in his flagon, "Lately."

Anxious now, Bailey tries to say, *Not so lately, sir. Dark Enduring has always been much respected in Settle's Crossways.* But Black rubs at his left forearm, and words flounder in Bailey's mind. He does not intervene as Black asks without turning to regard the speaker, "Lately?" Black's manner suggests no particular interest.

The speaker is lean as a stick. His bare arms have the rope-like muscles and deep brown of a farmhand. He carries no weight on his frame, and his features droop like a hound's as he drinks. To Black he smells of sweat and grievance. His name is Trait, and if he is asked, he will say that he is bitter because the town's prosperity has passed him by. But that is not Black's question. Trait takes a long pull at his flagon, then says, "Since the murder."

Now Bailey intends to intervene in earnest. Several of his patrons have heard Trait, and a stillness comes over the room. Soon everyone will be listening. But Black continues to rub his forearm, and Bailey scowls because he cannot remember what he wants to say.

Black does not ask about the murder. He will learn what he needs to know soon enough. Instead he asks, "And that encourages attendance at the Temple of Dark Enduring? How so?"

Bailey contrives to blurt, "You are a religious man, sir?" But Black and Trait ignore him.

"That priest," Trait says. He frowns. "What is his name?" Then he remembers. "Father Tenderson. He says what we want to hear."

Black lifts his hand to Bailey, points at Trait's flagon. Bailey understands. He refills the flagon at an ale-tap and replaces it in front of Trait.

Still revealing no great interest, Black asks, "What do you want to hear?"

Trait gulps at his drink for a moment. Then he says with satisfaction, "Revenge. Retribution.

"That other priest. Father Whorry. He promises glory. He preaches that poor Jon Marker's boy is with Bright Eternal, all light and happiness. He says if we have faith what we lose will not grieve us. Who takes comfort in slop like that? Father Tenderson speaks truth."

From somewhere behind Black, a man calls out, "Enough, Trait. He is a stranger. He has his own concerns. Jon Marker's loss means nothing to him."

Trait grins sourly. He enjoys the reprimand. It makes him more substantial in his own eyes. "Father Tenderson," he tells Black more distinctly, "demands punishment. He prays every day for the King's Justice. He wants the man who butchered that boy burned alive." He knocks his flagon on the bar. "We all do. We pray for the same thing." Again he claps the bar with his flagon. "Revenge will comfort us."

Then he snorts more quietly, "Glory will not."

Black does not say, The King's Justice is not what that priest thinks it is. Instead he remarks, "Father Whorry sounds judicious. He values peace." Then he asks, "Can a stranger meet with him? I, too, value peace." His tone is noncommittal. "Does he frequent a tavern of an evening?"

The man behind Black responds loudly, "The good Father will be at his prayers. Settle's Crossways is his concern. Wait for the morrow, stranger. Your desire to accost him at such a time is unseemly."

Black does not apologize. While he considers his reply, Trait mutters into his flagon, "At his prayers, aye—if they belong in a common house. If not, he labors for peace by other means."

"*Enough*, Trait," commands the man behind Black again. He

approaches the bar. "Is this a fit occasion for your spite?" He slaps a heavy hand on Trait's shoulder. "Show respect, man, for Jon Marker if you have none for the priest."

Trait smirks into his flagon, but does not retort.

The man rounds on Black. "Do you mean to mock us, sir?" he demands. He is large, granite-browed, and muscular. His apparel suggests wealth by its fineness, and indeed he owns a well-stocked general store. Others consider him a bully, but he believes himself a man often justly offended—and able to act against insult. "Our concerns are none of yours."

Knowing the man, Bailey hastens to placate him. "Be easy, Ing Hardiston," he says in his most soothing voice. "This is a trying time at its best. A stranger might well give offense without the intent to do so."

Black ignores the barkeep. He faces Hardiston's anger. Still disinterested in his manner, he says, "Father Tenderson, then. Is *he* a drinking man?"

Trait stifles a guffaw with ale.

Ing Hardiston bristles. He has blows in mind. Like many another man, he fears for his sons, and his fear incenses him. He desires to deny that he is afraid. But Black's lightless gaze weakens him. Though he clenches his fist, he does not swing.

Casting a glare at Bailey, the storekeeper then returns to Black. "Ask him yourself, sir," he says with knotted jaws, "when you see him on the morrow. You will not trouble the folk of this town at night."

Black does not acquiesce. Nor does he refuse. He has taken

Ing Hardiston's measure and is not threatened. Rather than prolong the man's ire, he turns to Trait.

"Will you guide me to an inn, friend? I am unquestionably a stranger. Without aid, I may find myself in a flea-ridden bed when I prefer comfort."

For a moment, Trait hesitates. He enjoys his ability to vex Hardiston and is inclined to do as Black asks. Like the storekeeper, however—and Bailey as well—he finds the stranger's aspect discomfiting. Conflicting impulses keep him silent until he recalls that the stranger has bought him ale.

In a long draught, Trait empties his flagon. Then he nods to Black. "I will." Shouldering Hardiston discourteously aside, he stands from his stool.

Rasping an oath, Ing Hardiston returns to his table and his companions.

When Black also stands, Bailey rallies himself to request payment. He goes so far as to meet Black's gaze. However, what he sees there closes his mouth. Flapping one hand, he dismisses the question of coin. At the last, he manages only to wish Black a pleasant night.

Black nods gravely. "Perhaps it will be pleasant," he replies. Then he accompanies Trait from the tavern.

But he has no interest in a bed. His purpose requires him to trace the smell of evil to its source, and he has come no nearer since entering the town. His interactions in the tavern have not awakened his glyphs and sigils, his scarifications. A few steps along the porch, he halts his companion.

Full night has come to Settle's Crossways. The town's many lamps dim the stars, but those lights are too earthbound to obscure the now-cloudless sweep of the heavens. Briefly Black studies the dulled jewels of darkness past the eaves of the roof, though he has no need of their counsel. To Trait, he says, "Take me to Jon Marker's house."

Trait stares. He finds Black difficult to discern in the shadows. He will say, You asked for an inn. He will refuse Black's command. He will pretend obedience to the storekeeper's wishes. Though he has neither wife nor son himself, he has still some kindness in him, and he is disturbed by Jon Marker's loss. He will not comply with Black.

He does comply. He wants more ale. His mouth hangs open as he points to an alley across the street.

Together, Black and his guide cross the street. The alley takes them to a lesser street, a crooked way aimless to those who do not know the town. Here the odor Black seeks teases his nose, but it remains indistinct, not to be trusted. He does not release Trait.

Another alley admits them to a still-smaller street. Away from the main roads, there is no gravel to give purchase. Black's boots squish and slip in the mud. Trait moves unsteadily, wishing himself back at the tavern, but the inconvenience of poor footing does not compel Black's attention. He follows his nose and his companion to a house that stands pressed close to its neighbors.

The place is little more than a hut large enough for perhaps three rooms. Its size and humility suggest that its occupants are poor. Yet there are no sprung boards in its walls, no gaps around its windows. Its porch and roofs are solid. All have been painted in a recent season. The chairs on the porch, where a husband and wife might sit of a quiet evening, are comfortable. To Black, it has the air of a dwelling cared for because its people consider it a home.

But its neighbors have lanterns on their porches and lights in their windows. The house to which Black has come is dark. It looks empty. In another season or two, it will look abandoned.

"Here," Trait says. Then he finds the kindness to add, "Let poor Jon be. He is a good man. Good men are few."

Black dismisses his guide. He forgets Trait. He is on the trail. The smell is stronger here. It is not strong enough to be the source he seeks. Still it confirms that he is on the right path.

The scent is not that of human violence, of ordinary passion or greed too extreme to be controlled. For such a crime, Settle's Crossways would not need the King's Justice. The smell is that of shapers and wicked rituals.

Silent as shadows, Black ascends the porch to the door.

For a moment, he considers his purpose. Then he knocks. He is sure that the house is not empty.

After a second knock, he hears boots on bare boards. They shuffle closer. At another time, perhaps, he will feel sorrow for the man inside. At present, his purpose rules him.

When the door opens, he sees a small man much blurred by what has befallen him. His eyes are reddened in the gloom, and his gaze is vague, like that of a man deep in his cups, though he does not smell of ale or hard spirits. His sturdy, workman's frame has collapsed in on itself, making him appear smaller than he is.

He blinks at Black, uncertain of his ability to distinguish the stranger in the gloom. When he speaks, his voice is raw with expended sobs. He says only, "What?"

Black stands motionless. "Are you a temple-going man, Jon Marker?" he asks. "Do you find ease in sermons and worship?"

Perhaps that is why or how his son was chosen.

Jon Marker repeats, "What?" He does not understand the question. Then he does. "Go. Leave me alone. I do not deal with hypocrites. Let others pretend to worship gods who do not answer prayers. I am not such a fool."

Perhaps *that* is why his son was chosen.

Jon Marker tries to close the door. Even in grief, he is too polite to slam it. But Black stops him. Gently Black says, "Then I must look elsewhere." He smells no atrocity on the man, or in the house. The odor he seeks is here by inference, indirectly. It lingers with its victims when its source has moved on. "I need your guidance. Tell me of your son."

Now the door is shut, though Jon Marker does not close it. He and Black stand in the common room of the house, on uncovered floorboards, in darkness. Jon Marker blinks more rapidly, but his sight does not clear.

The stranger wants him to speak of his son. The command angers him. It was not a request, despite its gentleness. "I will not," he answers. His pain is too raw.

"You will," Black replies, still gently. "I require your aid."

———

Jon Marker gathers himself to shout. He gathers himself to lay hands on the stranger. But under his cloak, Black rubs a glyph near the small of his back with one hand. With the other, he reaches out to cup his inlaid palm to Jon Marker's cheek.

Jon Marker tries to flinch away, yet he does not.

Black's touch enters the father's ruin. It does not give comfort. It is deeper than consolation. It brings a wail from the depths of Jon Marker's heart.

"My son!"

Soft as the night's air, Black says, "Tell me."

For a moment, the father cannot. His wail holds him, though he does not repeat it. It echoes in the empty frame that his home and his family have become. But then he answers in broken chunks like pieces of his flesh torn from him.

"When my wife, my sweet wife. My Annwin. When she died. When the plague claimed her. She took it all. All of me. I thought she took it all. The plague—" His voice catches. "I could not endure my life.

"But I could. She left my boy. Our son, our Tamlin. As sweet to me as she was. As kind. As pleasant. As willing. And lost." His voice fills the dark room with ghosts. "As lost as I was. We were lost together. Without her, lost. Until he found himself for me. Or I found myself for him. Or we found each other. Together, we found—

"It was *cruel*. Cruel to me. Cruel to him. That we had to go on without her smiles. But his kindness. His sweetness. His willingness. He was a reason to go on. And he needed a reason, as lost as I was. And I loved him. With whatever I had left, I loved him. I tried to be his reason."

Quiet as the vanished sound of Jon Marker's wail, Black says, "Your love was enough. You saved him. His love saved you. Tell me."

With Black's palm on his cheek, Jon Marker becomes stronger. "I earned our way serving in Ing Hardiston's store. With Annwin to tend our home, and Tamlin laughing in his chores at her side, I did not chafe at Hardiston's harsh ways. But after the plague—" The man remembers anger. "Ing Hardiston has no patience for grief. I was dismissed, and lost, and could not earn our way. Also folk avoided us, thinking the plague clung to us still. Thinking us cursed."

A faint whisper, Black says again, "Tell me."

"But Father Whorry—" Jon Marker swallows a lump of woe and gratitude. "He is a priest and a hypocrite. He is known for whoring. But he has kindness in him. He persuaded Haul Varder the wheelwright to employ me. Lying, he told Varder I had been sanctified when I had not, and was therefore certainly free of plague. Free of curse.

"And Haul Varder also is kind, in his rough way. He did not fault me for keeping Tamlin at my side while I worked, though my boy was too small to do more than sweep the floor. Without knowing what he did, Varder helped us find each other, Tamlin and me."

Black is not impatient, but his purpose has its own demands. Still touching Jon Marker's cheek, he goes further.

"Tell me of the murder."

Jon Marker cannot refuse. "A terrible day came," he says while his whole body cringes. "A day like any other. The work was hard, but hard work is good, and my boy was goodness itself. As much goodness as my Annwin left in the world. When the day was ending, I told Tamlin to hurry home to fire the stove for supper. We had promised each other some hours of play when we had eaten." Again he swallows, but now the lump in his throat is anger at himself. It is weeping for his boy. "*I* sent him home. I sent him *alone*. The fault is mine.

"I did not find him again until he had been slaughtered. He was not in the house. The stove was cold. I searched for him, crying his name. I roused my neighbors. Some searched with me. We did not find him until we looked near the refuse-pit behind the houses. He had been discarded—" A third time, his pain chokes him until he swallows it. "What remained of him had been thrown in the pit."

There Black lowers his hand. He feels pity, but he does not take pity. He has heard enough. Soon he will learn more of what he needs to know.

When he releases Jon Marker, the man collapses. But Black catches him, holds him upright. "Be easy," Black tells him. "We are almost finished. Show me where your son is buried. Then you will be done with me. For my life, I will ask nothing more."

Jon Marker thinks that he has fainted. Still he hears Black clearly. Fearing even now for those he has lost, he summons the strength to turn his head. In a voice that has been scraped until it bleeds, he asks, "Will you dig up my sweet boy? Will you be so cruel? After all that he has suffered?"

"I must see the place," Black answers. He means that he must touch and smell it. "But I will only disturb his body if you do not tell me what was done to him."

He will not coerce Jon Marker again, though he has many forms of influence ready for his use, and some Tamlin's father will not feel. This restraint is how he expresses pity.

Jon Marker is angry now, as angry as he was when he buried his son. "Bastard," he pants, this man whose wife loved him for his mildness, his gentleness, his natural courtesy. "Whoreson."

"Even so," Black replies. He feels no insult. There is no vexation in his heart. "I do what I do because I must."

Jon Marker stands away from Black. He knots his fists. "He was *beaten*!" he shouts. No words can express the force inside him. The house is too small to hold it. "Beaten *terribly*, damn you! Worse than any dog. Worse than any slave among the caravans. But he was still alive—the healer thinks he was still *alive*—when he was cut from gullet to groin. If I believed in gods and prayer, I would pray that he died before his lungs and *liver* were taken."

Lungs, Black thinks, and liver. Lungs for air. Liver for heat. Air and heat are elemental energies, as natural and necessary as bright and dark. But they do not cause imbalance, they played no part in the Balance Wars, because no shaper in the known world can draw upon them. They are everywhere and nowhere, too diffuse to offer power. Therefore they have neither temples nor priests.

He does not understand why the boy was butchered in this fashion. There are no rituals for air and heat. But he can guess now why Tamlin Marker was chosen. The boy's father has told him enough for that.

The how of the choosing remains uncertain. Black can speculate, but he does not commit himself.

"I have caused you pain," he tells Jon Marker. "Accept my thanks. Show me your son's grave. I will not disturb it. Nor will I disturb you again."

Jon Marker's anger drains from him as swiftly as it swelled. He thinks that he has come to the end of himself. He is as empty as the house. He does not speak. Instead he shuffles to the door, opens it, and waits for the stranger to precede him.

When Black walks out into the night, Jon Marker is with him.

The man stays on the neighboring porches until they end. Then he moves into the street, taking Black toward the outskirts of Settle's Crossways. Briefly Black considers that Jon Marker will lead him to a cemetery, but soon he recognizes his error. The town has suffered a plague. There will be a bare field like a midden where the victims are buried. Tamlin may be among them. Some of the townsfolk believed that the disease clung to him. And likely many of the bodies were burned, a precaution against the spread of infection. No doubt the evil Black smells

---

wished the same for Tamlin, to conceal the crime. Still Black is certain that Tamlin was not burned. He is certain that the boy's father would not permit it.

He and Jon Marker trudge through mire to the edge of the town. They leave the fading street to cross a long stretch of sodden grasses. Beyond it, they come to the field Black expects, an acre or more of churned mud where ashes and bones and bodies were covered in haste.

At the field's verge, Jon Marker pauses, but he does not stop. Awkward on the torn slop of the earth, he slogs to the far side. Then he goes farther to enter among the first trees of the forest. There he guides Black to a small glade with a mound of soaked dirt at its center. Between the trees, he has provided his son with the dignity of a separate grave, a private burial. When he nears the mound, wavering on his feet, he says only, "Here." Then he drops to his knees and bows his head.

Again Black says, "Accept my thanks." He, too, kneels. But he does so in the sloping mud of the grave. He places his hands on the mound and works his fingers into the dirt as deep as his wrists. After a moment, he closes his eyes. With all of his senses, he concentrates on the scent he seeks.

The rain has washed much away. In addition, the forest is rich with its own smells. And Tamlin's burial is at least a fortnight old. Black knows this because so many days have passed since he first began to track the smell of wickedness. But he has sigils for keenness and glyphs for penetration. The odor that compels him is distinct. He needs only moments to be certain that he has not misled himself with Tamlin Marker's death. He feels the truth of what Jon Marker has told him.

He recognizes the ritual, and does not recognize it. His thoughts become urgent, goaded by the discrepancy between what he expects and what surprises him.

Why was the boy beaten? Because he fought. Because his killer enjoyed hurting him. But that explanation does not account for the murder itself.

Still kneeling, he lifts his hands from the dirt. "It is not enough," he says, unaware that he speaks aloud. "One child, yes. An innocent boy. A beautifully innocent boy. But it is not enough for power. It does not enable sorcery. He is the start of a ritual, or he is its end. There must be others. Several others. Perhaps many others."

Jon Marker says, "There are no others," but Black does not heed him. Black is already certain that none of the townsfolk have been butchered as Tamlin was. The people he has met would react differently if they knew themselves threatened. The guards on the road would be more stringent in their duty, more numerous. Also the source of this evil needs secrecy until the ritual is ripe.

"They will be brutal men," he thinks, still aloud. "Men who relish harming innocence. Or cruel women who relish it."

He is sure of this, just as he is sure that the lungs and livers of the other corpses have been taken. Yet he does not understand it. Shapers do not pursue the impossible. They cannot draw their sorcery from air and heat.

———

Tamlin's father makes a sound of distress, but Black does not attend to it. He is immersed in his confusion. If his words have wounded Jon Marker, he does not regard the cost.

Still he is a veteran. He has fought many battles, he bears many scars, and he has been shaped for his task. His instincts are sure. Despite his concentration, he feels the men coming. As lightly as mist and shadows, he rises to meet them.

There is no moon to light the glade. Only the stars define the shapes of the trees. Yet Black sees clearly. Some of his sigils are awake. Some of his scarifications burn. He recognizes Ing Hardiston as the storekeeper approaches. The two other men he does not know. But one of them holds a longknife to Jon Marker's throat. The other advances a dozen paces to Hardiston's left. This man holds his cutlass ready. The storekeeper is armed with a heavy saber.

Black sighs. He knows that these men have no bearing on his purpose. He does not want to kill them. Under his cloak, he rubs his left forearm.

The man gripping Jon Marker lowers his longknife. The man with the cutlass hesitates. But Ing Hardiston strides forward. Though his fear is strong, his loathing of it—or of himself—is stronger. His anger shrugs aside Black's attempt to confuse him.

"You were warned, stranger," the storekeeper snarls. "You meddle where you are not wanted. It is time for you to die." His saber cuts the air. "If Marker is the cause of your coming, he has lived too long."

Hardiston's example restores his men. The longknife is again ready at Jon Marker's throat. The cutlass rises for its first stroke.

"Now you also are warned," Black replies. He is more vexed than irate. This interruption is worse than foolish. It is petty. "Jon Marker has suffered much, and I have refreshed his pain. I will permit no further harm to him."

When he touches his hip with his left hand, his longsword appears in his right. Its slim blade swarms with sigils for sharpness and glyphs for strength. Its tip traces invocations in the night.

Again the man with the cutlass hesitates. This time, he is shaken by surprise rather than slowed by confusion.

Ing Hardiston also hesitates. He yelps a curse. But his need to deny his fear is greater than his surprise. His curse becomes a howl as he charges.

Black is one with the darkness. His movements are difficult to discern as he tangles Hardiston's saber with his cloak. A flick of his longsword severs the tendons of Hardiston's wrist. In the same motion, his elbow crumples Hardiston's chest. As the storekeeper hunches and falls, too stunned to understand his own pain, Black spins behind him.

A flash in the night, Black's longsword leaves his hand. It impales the thigh of the man holding a blade to open Jon Marker's throat. The impact and piercing cause a shriek as the man topples away from Tamlin's father.

Black has no wish to kill any of these men. Unarmed, he

confronts the man with the cutlass. In a voice of silk, he asks, "Do you require a second warning?"

For a moment, the man stares. Then he drops his weapon and runs, leaving his fellows bloody on the grass.

When Black sees Jon Marker prone beside his writhing attacker, the veteran is truly vexed. He is on the trail and means to follow it. Yet he cannot forsake the man who has aided him. Moving swiftly, he retrieves his longsword and causes it to disappear. Then he stoops to examine Jon Marker.

He sighs again as he finds the man unhurt. Jon Marker is only prostrate with exhaustion. All his wounds are within him, where Black cannot tend them. Still Black gives what care he can. Lifting the unconscious man in his arms, Black carries him back to his empty house. There he settles Jon Marker in the nearest bed.

Though Black's purpose urges him away, he watches over the man who has helped him until dawn.

～∾

With the night's first waning, Black leaves Jon Marker asleep and returns to the stables where he bedded his horse.

The mount that awaits him there is altered since the previous evening. The ostler remarks on this as he hands the reins to Black. "Much changed he is, sir," the man says, "much changed. A different horse, I judged, that I did. A substitute for your sorry nag. Some fool plays a trick on me. But look, sir. The markings are the same. The scars here and here." The man points. "The white fetlocks. The notched ears. Notched like sword-cuts they are, sir. And the tack. I am not mistaken, sir, I swear it. There is no accounting for it. Rest and water and good grain are not such healers."

Black's only response is a nod. He has no reason for surprise. His mount has been shaped to meet his needs, as he has. For his long journey, and to enter the town, he required an aged and weary steed that would attract no notice, suggest no wealth. Now he means to travel with speed. The distance may be considerable. Also he may encounter opposition, though he does not expect it. Thus his mount must be a stallion trained for fleetness in battle, and so it has become.

When he has saddled his horse, tightened the girth, and swayed the ostler to refuse payment, he mounts and rides.

While he passes through Settle's Crossways, retracing the street that brought him here, he goes at a light canter, though the dawn is still grey, and he encounters few folk early to their tasks. Once he leaves the sleep-stunned guards behind, however, he gallops hard. He hopes to return before the morning is gone.

A league into the forest, he halts. For a time, he studies the air on both sides of the road with his sharpened senses. Then he turns his horse to enter among the trees and deep brush, heading east.

Though he has no cause to remember it, he has not forgotten

the lonely mountain that fumes over Settle's Crossways in this direction.

Through the close-grown trees and the tangled obstructions of brush, creepers, and fallen deadwood, he makes what haste he can. For the moment, he seeks only a path, one seldom trodden. A deer-track will suffice. When he finds one, he goes more swiftly.

The trail wanders, as such things do, yet he does not doubt his choice. Within half a league, the vague whiff that he detected from the roadside becomes more intelligible. It is still faint, obscured by wet loam and dripping leaves and passing animals. The rain masked it while he rode toward Settle's Crossways the previous day. Also it is diluted by time and other odors. Nevertheless it is the scent of his quarry's rituals. Sure of his discernment, he follows it.

His mount canters dangerously among the trees. It leaps in stride over fallen boles, intruding boulders, slick streams. Sunrise slanting through the forest catches Black's eyes in quick glints and sudden shafts, but he lowers the brim of his hat and rides on.

The smell of wild beasts grows stronger, and also a growing reek of rot. Abruptly he enters a clearing. It is well hidden, and he sees that a number of men have lived there. Perhaps they had women with them. Several sturdy shelters more elaborate than lean-tos stand at the edges of the open space. Discarded garments and bundles litter the ground. Among them he sees a short sword, several truncheons, an empty quiver. He does not need to look in order to know that the shelters once held stores of food, of meat and bread. These have been much ravaged by animals, but the decay of the remains informs him of their former presence.

In the center of the clearing is a wide fire-pit, its ashes sodden and cold. It has been abandoned for many days, more than a fortnight. And the corpse sprawled among the ashes has also been abandoned. Most of its flesh has been torn from the bones, the bones themselves have been cracked and gnawed, and the scraps of its motley garments lie scattered around the pit. The mangling of the body prevents Black from knowing whether the lungs and liver were taken intact. Still the scent that he seeks is strong here, despite the putrid sweetness of rot. He does not doubt that he is looking at another ritual murder.

The crime is old, but its age does not prevent him from imagining the scene. A band of brigands made this clearing their home. After their attacks on caravans and wagons, they returned here, hid here. But one night a man or men killed one of their sentries among the trees. When the lungs and liver were taken, and the man—no, the men—were ready, they burst into the clearing. They discarded their victim on the fire. By force of arms, or perhaps by mere surprise, they scattered the brigands.

And then—?

Black adjusts his senses to ignore the miasma of decay and feeding. He walks his horse once around the clearing, twice. Then he picks a faint track similar to the one that brought him here and follows it.

Within a hundred paces, he finds a second corpse. Hidden in the brush to his left, he discovers a third. Both are old and badly ravaged. He cannot determine how or why they were killed. Still the smell of evil clings to them. Studying them with a veteran's eye in the rising daylight, he concludes that both died the same night their sentry was cast into the fire.

He suspected the truth earlier. Now he is sure. The butchering of innocence is the end of the ritual, not the start. Therefore he is also sure that the culmination of the crimes, the completion of their purpose, will be soon.

Because he does not understand that purpose, he cannot guess why it was not acted upon immediately after Tamlin Marker's death. Still he believes that he has little time. He is reassured only by the knowledge that three men and a boy are not enough.

But half a league deeper in the forest, he finds a fourth corpse—and after another half-league, the shredded remains of three women tossed into the pit left by the falling of a dead tree. The count now stands at seven. If it reaches ten, it will be enough, if the ritual is of a kind that Black knows. If it climbs still higher, he will be in serious danger.

It does not stop at ten. Eventually he locates seven more bodies, men and women, all brigands by their apparel and weapons. Their odor tells him that their deaths are more recent than the first seven. In two instances, the condition of the corpses allows him to see that the lungs and livers have been harvested.

To himself, Black acknowledges that the perpetrator of this ritual is clever. Brigands who raid from coverts are ideal victims. Their absence will be noticed with gratitude. The reason for their absence will interest no one.

Alarmed now, he suspects that if he wanders the woods around Settle's Crossway for days, he will find a number of similar deaths. Some will be older than those he has already found. Perhaps some will be more recent. The source of this evil is growing stronger. Its intent must be extreme, if it requires such bloodshed. Why else has its culmination been delayed?

He judges, however, that he cannot afford to search farther. Unseen events are accumulating. Incomprehensible purposes gather against Settle's Crossways, or against the kingdom itself. He must try to forestall them.

With as much haste as his horse can manage, he returns to the road. Then he gallops back toward the town like a man with hounds and desperation on his heels.

But he does not reenter Settle's Crossways on the road. He is unwilling to be delayed by the guards, and he has no wish to silence them with sterner persuasions than he used the previous evening. Leaving the road, he returns to the glade where Tamlin Marker is buried, then re-crosses the plague-midden to reach Jon Marker's house by its neglected street.

There he does not pause to trouble the wounded father again. He loops his horse's reins around one of the roof-posts of the porch, knowing that his mount will remain until he needs it. Unaffected by the mud underfoot, he strides by streets and alleys toward the town's center.

At the crossroads where the temples of Bright Eternal and

Dark Enduring face each other, comfortable in their proximity, Black finds good fortune. A modest caravan is dragging its clogged wheels toward the town square from the west, and already the streets teem with merchants and townsfolk, hawkers and mountebanks, some surely hoping to buy what they lack, others intending to both buy and sell, still others striving to gull the unwary. Also the caravan will have its own needs for resupply. Therefore Black is sure that the wagons, their owners, their drivers, and their guards will remain in the square for some time. Since noon is near, they will likely remain until the morrow. He will have opportunities to speak with the caravan-master later.

Rubbing his left forearm, he sways a distracted matron to direct him to Father Whorry's dwelling. She is a milliner, avid to purchase fine fabrics and threads from one wagon or another before her competitors acquire them, but she forgets her hurry briefly in order to answer Black. Then she rejoins the surge of the crowd.

Black separates himself from the townsfolk, touching his hat to everyone who gazes at him directly. Then he follows the matron's instructions.

The priest's residence is a mansion compared to Jon Marker's house, yet it is humble enough to suit the servant of a god. Like every other dwelling that Black has seen here, it has a wide porch linked to its neighbors' to provide passage safe from the sludge and traffic of the streets. The door has only an emblazoned yellow symbol, a stylized sun, to indicate that this is the home of a

Bright priest. Black knocks politely, though he senses that the house is empty.

But Father Whorry is already hastening homeward after a night in his preferred common house. He is a small man, rotund, with an anxious smile on his round face and a few long wisps of hair on his pate. He wears the brown cassock and yellow chasuble of his office, and might therefore be expected to walk with dignity. However, he clings to the notion that all Settle's Crossways does not know of his pleasure with women, and so his movements have an air of furtiveness as he attempts to pass unnoticed.

When he gains the privacy of his residence, he closes the door quickly, then sighs and slumps before turning to discover a stranger waiting for him in the gloom of the unlighted lamps.

Father Whorry aspires to a priest's imperturbable calm, but he cannot stifle a startled gasp as he regards the stranger. For a moment, his legs threaten to fail him.

"Father Whorry?" Black's tone is pitched to reassure this servant of Bright Eternal. "I must speak with you."

At once, the priest begins to babble, an incoherent spate of words to fill the silence while he struggles to recapture his wits. However, the stranger rubs his left forearm, and Father Whorry's alarm fades. When the stranger says, "You do not lock your door, Father. I took that for an invitation. Was I mistaken?" the priest has a reply ready, though he speaks too quickly for dignity.

"No, of course not, of course not, my son. All are welcome.

You are welcome. I am considered a servant of Bright Eternal, but in fact I serve all who hold our god in their hearts." He intends to ask the stranger's name, but the question escapes him. Instead he asks, "You wish to speak with me?"

Black pretends to smile under the brim of his hat. "I do." His voice is soothing silk. Beneath the scents of women, wine, and sweat, Father Whorry smells as innocent as a bathed babe. "But since I must put the same questions to Father Tenderson as well, we will spare ourselves effort and time if I speak to him and you together. Will you accompany me?"

Staring, Father Whorry manages to say, "Father Tenderson? He is an apostate. A former son of Bright Eternal. There is no truth in him." But the way the stranger rubs his forearm is unaccountably calming, and the priest has no difficulty adding, "But of course, of course. We are friends, that old blackguard and I. Bright Eternal forgives even those who do not wish it." He is pleased by the quality of his own smile. "Shall we go?"

Black touches Father Whorry's arm as though he, too, is the priest's friend. He guides Father Whorry from the house in a way that allows the small man to lead him.

Explaining that the crowds in the square will make passage there impossible, Father Whorry takes Black by side-streets and alleys to a residence that closely resembles his own. Of its external details, the only significant difference is that the symbol emblazoned on the door is a stylized stroke of lightning entirely black. Here, however, the windows are warm with lamplight, and a flicker at one of the panes suggests a fire in the hearth.

The Bright priest ascends the porch without hesitation. He is often a guest here, more often than he entertains his apostate friend. Father Tenderson's home is more comfortably furnished, and the Dark priest serves better wine. Father Whorry knocks on the emblem of Dark Enduring and waits at ease for an answer, sure of his welcome.

Black hears slippered feet on a rug before Father Tenderson opens the door, spilling light and good cheer over the arrivals.

The Dark priest is a tall man, and too lean to disguise the old sorrow in his soul. Yet his sadness does not mar him. His long face crinkles with ready smiles, the pleasure in his eyes promises easy laughter, and his open arms are full of greeting. Unlike his Bright friend, he would have hair aplenty on his head, though much grizzled, if he did not wear it cropped short.

In appearance, he is an odd man to urge vengeance and the King's Justice. But his preaching arises from bitter disappointment as well as deep grieving, from too much experience of pettiness and spite, and from more personal losses. For that reason, he believes, his words touch the hearts of many townsfolk. He gives them the only comfort he knows. And when he has preached with the eloquence of his own pain, he resumes the cheerfulness that is his nature.

"Father Whorry!" he exclaims. "And a stranger. Enter!" He stands aside with a sweep of his arm. "Enter and be welcome. I cannot feed you. It is early for my noonday meal. Nothing is prepared. But wine I have, and my fire is too good for one man alone."

Father Whorry ducks his head to enter, then raises it as he embraces his friend. He feels stronger in Father Tenderson's presence, as he often does, and now considers himself better able to face the stranger.

Father Tenderson pats his nominal opponent's head affectionately, then turns his gaze on the hatted and cloaked stranger. "And you are, sir? I believe I have heard mention of your arrival yesterday, but I do not know your name."

It is Black's immediate intention to sound ominous, to suggest threats. "My name is of no use to you." He has brought the priests together because he hopes to provoke revelations. "It cannot command me." As he speaks, however, he smells only cleanliness on the Dark priest. Like his friend, Father Tenderson has no malice in him. By that sign, Black knows that he must alter his approach. Resuming his silken tone, he adds, "But for convenience, I am known as Black."

"Black you are," observes the Dark priest with merriment in his eyes, "and are not. Yet you are welcome by any name. Please." He gestures toward the hearth, where three well-cushioned armchairs and a settee are positioned to enjoy the fire. "Be seated. Will you accept wine?"

Father Whorry nods vigorously. Black shakes his head. While Father Tenderson moves to a cabinet at the side of the room, selects a fired clay flask, and fills three goblets of the same material, the Bright priest scurries to the farthest armchair, hoping to put as much distance as he can between himself and Black.

Ignoring both men, Black seats himself upon the settee. It is too close to the fire for comfort, but he does not regard the warmth.

Carrying three goblets on a tray, the Dark priest offers one to Father Whorry. Black again declines in silence. "Should you change your mind," Father Tenderson suggests as he places the tray on the rug near the settee. Taking a goblet for himself, he settles his long limbs into the nearest armchair.

Black has much to consider. If he does not procure revelations by menace, he must use other means. And he suspects that the simple suasion he has used on Father Whorry will not prompt the honesty he requires. Also he believes that he will gain nothing by the form of coercion he imposed on Jon Marker. Answers he will get, but they will only be as useful as his questions, and he does not know enough to ask the right questions.

He remains silent until Father Tenderson says, "Now, Black. Father. You are here together for some purpose. Let us speak of it before my housekeeper's bustle interrupts us."

This opening surprises Father Whorry. He is easily flustered, but he is also familiar with the Dark priest's usual manner. He expects his friend to commence with casual inquiries to set the stranger at ease. Where are you from? What brings you to Settle's Crossways? And so forth. Father Tenderson's forthrightness makes the Bright priest's eyebrows dance surprise on his brow.

"Very well," begins Black. "You are aware, I hope, that you are both charlatans."

The priests stare, Father Whorry anxiously, Father Tenderson with wry sadness.

Black does not speak as he does to insult his listeners. Rather he attempts to shift the ground under their feet. If he succeeds, he may elicit replies that would escape him otherwise.

"You worship gods," he explains. "You encourage others in the same worship. Yet you are old enough to have some memory of a time when there were no temples. If you are not, your fathers were. In those days, no one imagined bright and dark as gods. They were known for what they are, elemental energies, nothing more. They exist, and they are mighty. But they are mindless. They do not think, or care, or answer. They are no more worthy of worship, and no less, than wind and sunlight."

Frowning now, Father Tenderson leans forward, his elbows on his knees, to give this visitor his full attention. Black's gaze stops a protest in Father Whorry's mouth. The Bright priest gulps wine to appease his indignation.

"There are four elemental energies," Black continues, "all potent. Together they make life possible in the world. But of the four, only bright and dark are accessible to shapers." When he sees that the word perplexes the priests, he says, "You may know such people as sorcerers. They have the knowledge and the means to draw power from one or the other, bright or dark. And when they draw power from one, they make the other commensurately stronger. They create an imbalance.

"It is true to say that the elemental energies make life possible, but it is also incomplete. The full truth is more fragile. It is both the energies themselves and the balance among them that enable life. Individually they are each too mighty to be survived. Any imbalance among them is fatal. It threatens every aspect of the living world.

"So much you know. Your fathers did if you do not."

"Then why do you tell us?" asks Father Tenderson. But he speaks softly. He is not impatient for Black's answer.

"The balance must be preserved," Black replies. "This task the King has taken upon himself. When one shaper seeks advantage, or several do, by calling upon bright, the King counters by making use of dark. Or the reverse. Thus he mediates between them.

"Certainly you are old enough to remember the old wars, or to have heard tales." Black sighs. He remembers too much. "They were terrible in bloodshed. Many good lands were laid waste. And the forces that the shapers called upon grew in ferocity until the King contrived to become the mediator of balance. Until he imposed his peace on the kingdom.

"He cannot end the evil that lurks in the hearts of our kind, but he can prevent a recurrence of the old wars. He can and does."

Under his cloak, Black touches two sigils. He rests one hand in a place among his scarifications. He has not slept, and has eaten little. These invocations refresh his strength.

Again Father Tenderson asks, "Why do you tell us this?" Unlike Father Whorry, he is neither alarmed nor indignant. He has not tasted his wine. His curiosity is growing.

———

Black answers by completing his explanation.

"The King's mediation is an arduous task. It requires a more than human vigilance. And his reserves are not limitless. Also those who serve his will are few. Many were lost in the wars. For that reason, he named bright and dark gods, and he commanded temples for their worship. By so doing, he hoped to gain several forms of aid.

"First, he sought to make the communities of the kingdom stronger by uniting them in shared beliefs. Second, he desired the priests of his temples to teach respect for forces too great to be controlled. From respect, humility might grow, humility to counter the arrogance that encourages men and women to tamper with their gods. Last, he believed that worship itself might steady bright and dark. It might make them less susceptible to abuse."

Black gazes deeply into Father Tenderson. Drinking, Father Whorry avoids Black's scrutiny.

"I have named you charlatans," Black concludes, "and so you are. You encourage the folk of Settle's Crossways in false beliefs. But you are also the King's best servants here. Indeed, your service as it appears to me is flawless. You, Father Whorry, preach forgiveness, while you, Father Tenderson, demand the King's Justice. You balance each other. And you are friends. Together you lessen the peril of Bright Eternal and Dark Enduring."

Black shows the priests his open hands. Then he knots them together. "Still there is evil among you. Jon Marker's son was murdered by a shaper."

This is too much for Father Whorry. He cannot contain his anger longer. He cries, "Do you upbraid *us*, stranger?" Emptying his goblet, he slaps it upended to the rug so that his hands are free. "Are we accused?" His hands make fists that tremble as he raises them. "There are no shapers among us, none. We do not condone evil.

"When you say that they—these sorcerers—that they draw upon Bright Eternal or Dark Enduring for power, do you mean that they pray to their chosen god, and their prayers are answered? I do not preach that any god answers prayer. Father Tenderson does not. We mislead no one. I tell my flock only that their god accepts and pardons them, as he does all living things. Why must we doubt ourselves now? What have we to do with shapers and foul murder?"

Black means to pursue his needs, but Father Tenderson intervenes. Turning to the Bright priest, he urges gently, "Calm yourself, Father. Put your mind at rest. Black does not accuse us. Unless I am much mistaken, he has not named his reasons for bringing us together yet."

Then he faces Black once more. "Let us be clear, sir." There is no good cheer in him now. Though he considers himself cowardly, he has his own anger in addition to his sorrow, and they speak for him. "I do not boast when I say that neither of us would hesitate to stand between any child of Settle's Crossways and murder."

Black watches him in silence, waiting. He does not doubt what he hears, but it is not enough. Unfortunately he cannot teach the Fathers to recognize the smell he seeks. He cannot ask them about their parishioners.

After a moment, the Dark priest recalls that he has not been blamed, though he is quick to blame himself. Ruling his emotions sternly, he settles his sorrow back to its depths and his limbs in his chair.

"Our good Father Whorry's theology is simplicity itself," he begins. As he speaks, he recovers his composure. "His heart is pure. Therefore his service is pure. I take a more oblique view. Perhaps I spend too much time alone." He attempts a smile, then exchanges it for a rueful frown. "But leave that aside. I admire the King's efforts to provide peace. I am grateful to him. But I am not troubled by his reasons for creating our temples, and I am not diminished by my role as his charlatan.

"To my mind—Father Whorry will forgive me for repeating myself, we have argued the matter often enough—the faith is more necessary than the god. Worshipping together is more necessary than the god. And speaking what is in our hearts—as a form of worship, you understand—is more necessary than all else. Dark Enduring"—he raises a placating hand to his friend—"please, Father, I know your objections—is merely an excuse for wounded souls to come together so that they can say or hear what is in their hearts.

"The King, if I have understood you, sir, would not disapprove of either of us."

"He would not," Black confesses. He has his own faith. The Balance Wars must not be permitted to resume. He has faith in his purpose. "Still there is evil to consider. There is Tamlin Marker's murder to explain."

Father Whorry remains angry. "And you expect that of us? An explanation?"

Black shrugs. "You have knowledge of the townsfolk that I do not. Perhaps that will suffice.

"You know what was done to Jon Marker's boy?"

Father Tenderson nods with sadness in his eyes, but the Bright priest speaks first. "All Settle's Crossways knows."

"Do you also know how it chanced that Tamlin Marker was alone? That his killer was able to take him and remained unwitnessed?"

Now it is Father Tenderson who replies. "We have heard poor Jon's account. Directly or by rumor, we have heard it. He sent the boy home to fire the stove."

Black sits motionless as a stone. He reveals nothing. "And you do not call it *unlikely* that Tamlin's killer was ready to take him at the moment when mere chance provided his opportunity?"

Both men are struck by the question. They have not considered the matter in that light. Father Whorry's brows squirm. He rubs his hands together like a man attempting to wash away some stain. Father Tenderson stares with his eyes wide. He is too full of chagrin to contain it. When he speaks, his voice is hoarse.

"I call it unlikely *now*. Fool that I am, I did not think—" For a moment, he cannot continue. Then he asks, "How is such readiness possible? Do these shapers—?"

Black cuts him off. "No. Shapers are not seers. They do not

foresee. If they did, some among them would see cause for re-straint. The explanation I seek does not rely on sorcery."

"Then how?" demands Father Whorry. "It is impossible. How was it done?"

Black cannot answer. The priests must help him. He changes his approach.

"Jon Marker," he states, "lost his living in Ing Hardiston's store after his wife's passing." He does not tell the priests how he knows this. "You, Father Whorry, went to his aid. You found employment for him with a wheelwright named Haul Varder.

"But Jon Marker is not a temple-goer. He does not belong to your flock. Indeed, he scorns both temples and priests. How does it chance that you alone in Settle's Crossways sought to aid him?"

The Bright priest wants to shout a retort. He believes that now he is surely being accused. Yet he is out of his depth, and much of his anger is directed at himself. For that reason, he twists and cringes. How had he failed to grasp the unlikelihood of Tamlin Marker's taking? He has spent too much time besot-ted with wine and women. Though Black does not compel or confuse him, Father Whorry cannot refuse to answer.

"The man needed help." He is shamed by the smallness of his voice, or by his own smallness. "What else could I do? Bright Eternal does not discriminate. You say my god does not care. If that is true, it is also true that he does not judge. I offered Jon consolation, but he would not take it. Yet his need was severe. I did what I could."

To Black, Father Tenderson murmurs softly, "His service is pure. There is only kindness in his heart."

"And kindness in Haul Varder's," the Bright priest asserts more stoutly.

The taller man turns to his friend. Still softly, he urges, "Be honest, Father. Haul Varder is not known for kindness."

The Dark priest makes Father Whorry squirm. He feels driven to bluster. "His childhood was one of misery. All Settle's Crossways knows this. He did not learn kindness from his mother. Now his manner is dour and ungiving. What of it? He is known for self-interest, yes. He is much in demand, especially by caravans and wagoneers. But he could have readily found another to bend his iron and lathe his spokes. Settle's Crossways does not lack young men who want work. It was kindness that chose Jon Marker."

With the mildness of affection, Father Tenderson says, "More honest, Father."

The small man surprises himself by blurting an oath. Then he recants. "Bright Eternal forgive me." He speaks to his friend rather than to Black. "*More* honest? Well, if I must. For Tamlin Marker's sake.

"Haul Varder is also known for absences. He is commonly absent. If he did not have a good man to tend his forge and his iron, his business would founder.

"But"—Father Whorry sees a gleam of hope that he can win free of his friend's insistence—"he was present on the last day of Tamlin's life. The boy worked with his father, sweeping floors and such. Jon Marker would not have sent his son home without Haul Varder's leave. He is too courteous and diligent to be presumptuous with the man who pays his labor."

An instant later, the Bright priest claps his hand to his mouth as though he has just heard himself utter an obscenity. In his heart, he is crying, Bright Eternal! God forgive me! Have I *accused* Haul Varder?

Father Tenderson spreads his hands. To Black, he says, grieving, "You see how matters stand. I do not regard the wheelwright as charitably as my friend does. He bargains meanly for his services. He treats men who cannot pay with disdain. He has neither wife nor child, and does not regret his lack—or does not acknowledge that he regrets it. His absences are many. Some are prolonged. All are unexplained.

"Yet I also must be honest. I know no ill of the man. Like Jon Marker, he is no temple-goer, but that is not a fault in him."

There the Dark priest turns away. He gazes into the fire, searching the flames as he searches himself. "Father Whorry's kindness serves as courage. *I* did not aid Jon Marker. I had not the heart to approach that harmed man. His losses filled my veins with weakness.

"I talk and talk. My good friend occasionally bridles at my profusion of talk. But when I open myself to my god and my flock, I obscure more than I reveal. The truth is that I am weak. My friend is the better man. He is the better priest."

Black remains motionless. He considers what he has heard. He does not doubt either priest. They have given as much guidance as they possess, and it is more than they expect. Still he is baffled. He is both thoroughly shaped and well taught. His experience of sorcery, ambition, and greed is long by any measure. It has cost him pieces of his soul. Yet he knows of no ritual, even among those most vile, that requires lungs and livers. The King himself cannot draw upon air and heat.

Abruptly, Black stands. While his hosts scramble, surprised, to their feet, he says, "I have troubled you enough. A simpler question remains. Then I will disturb you no longer."

Father Whorry only gapes. He is much distressed, though less by what he has said than by what he has been caused to think. Against his will, he wonders whether he is culpable for Jon Marker's loss. He asks himself why he trusted Haul Varder's apparent kindness. Father Tenderson would not have committed that cruel error.

For his part, however, the Dark priest recovers from painful concerns more swiftly. He is practiced at submerging his anger and woe, his many regrets. Black has given him cause for consternation, but it does not stifle his native curiosity.

"Answer one query, sir, and I will answer yours," he replies with a semblance of his customary cheer. "You spoke of four elemental energies. Bright and Dark are two. What are the others?"

Black frowns. He finds that he does not wish to speak of such things. Naming them dismays him. It gives them a substance that he desires to deny.

Yet he is indebted to these men. Some debts he avoids when

he can, as Bailey, the barkeep, will attest. Others he repays in full. And on its face, Father Tenderson's inquiry is a small matter.

"They are air and heat," he replies, "as necessary as bright and dark. But they cause no concern. No shaper calls upon them. They are too diffuse. The knowledge to concentrate them does not exist."

He hopes that he speaks truth.

"Accept my thanks, sir," returns the Dark priest warmly. "I am edified. And your question?"

Black feels a need for haste that he cannot explain. "The caravan," he says. It has come from the west. Perhaps it comes from lands unknown to him. "I must speak with its master, but I do not know the town. Where do such men spend the night?"

Father Tenderson laughs. "Or women, in this case," he answers without hesitation. "Her name is Kelvera, though her men call her Blossom for obscure reasons. As for where she spends the night—" With a glance, he refers the question to his friend.

Lost in acid thoughts, Father Whorry names an inn without realizing that he is addressed or knowing that he answers.

Father Tenderson sees Black's desire to depart. In a few words, he directs Black to the inn. Then he says with wry mirth, "You will not think me rude, sir, if I do not escort you to the door. I am concerned for my friend. He needs the solace of more wine. I recognize the signs."

Black bows by inclining his head. Then he goes. Within himself he is running, though his stride is unhurried. He is sure of his ability to locate Haul Varder, but there are questions to which he desires answers before he approaches the wheelwright.

Among them is this. What use can a shaper make of lungs and livers? However, he does not expect to find an explanation in Settle's Crossways, or from any caravaner. Instead he hopes to understand a more practical matter.

How had one shaper attracted enough followers to kill so many brigands and suffer no losses without some rumor of those followers finding its way to the priests, or attaching itself to Haul Varder?

If the wheelwright is innocent, the shaper and his followers must have come to this region from a considerable distance— and must have contrived to remain entirely secret for an unlikely number of days.

Black means to go directly to the inn Father Whorry named. As he skirts the edges of the crowded square, however, he encounters the mother and daughter who addressed him when he first entered Settle's Crossways.

The mother's name is Rose, and she was widowed by the same plague that claimed Annwin Marker. For that reason, her anxiety for her fey daughter, Arbor, is greater than it was. And it has grown still greater since her meeting with the stranger. Her good husband had the gift of calming her. He saw no harm in little Arbor's real or imagined sight, and his unconcern eased Rose's heart. Without him, she has been troubled daily by the fear that her daughter's wits have strayed. But now she has a new fear. The stranger's belief that Arbor's sight is real is beyond her comprehension.

In Settle's Crossways, a town remote from the larger world, and ignorant apart from the gossip of wagoneers and caravaners, the gift of unnatural sight is not preferable to an unbalanced mind.

But Arbor is not afraid. During the past day, she has spoken often of the stranger with the holes in his soul, and of her desire to help him. She has insisted that she can heal his holes, one or more of them. Seeing him again excites her. While Rose flinches in alarm, Arbor succeeds in pulling free of her mother's hand. She runs toward the stranger as though she means to leap into his arms.

Black sees her. He sees her desire to touch him. But he also sees her mother's fear. And he has his own reasons for caution. He knows what may become of the girl if she aids him while she is too young to understand what she does. He holds up one hand while the other secretly invokes a sigil of command.

Surprised by herself, the girl stops.

Rose hastens closer. "Arbor!" she cries in a voice that trembles too much to sound stern. "He is a stranger. Leave him alone."

"But, Ma—" Arbor protests.

Still asserting his command, Black asks, "Your name is Arbor?" His tone is quiet reassurance.

The girl nods. She does not resist as her mother reclaims her hand.

Black meets the mother's wide stare. "And your name, madam?"

His command reaches her. Unwillingly, she replies, "Rose." But then she musters her resolve. "What have you to do with us, sir?" She aches for her husband's presence at her side. He would speak more confidently. "You called my daughter precious. I do not understand you. She is precious only to me."

Black nods. Soothing as water, he says, "Then hear me, Rose. Arbor has a gift for which I have no name. It is clear in her, though I cannot account for it. I am certain only that it is not ripe. When she is older, it will manifest more strongly, and more safely. For the present, it must not be spent on a stranger"—he gazes at Arbor ruefully—"even a stranger with holes in his soul." Then he faces Rose again. "But you are precious also. You have your own gift. You call it fear or grief, but it has other names.

"There is a man who needs your gifts, both yours and Arbor's. He is Jon Marker." Seeing Rose's bafflement, he adds, "You know of him. You know what he has lost. But perhaps you do not know that he is utterly alone.

"It would be a great kindness to befriend him."

If Arbor feels an impulse to touch Jon Marker's pain, she will do herself no harm.

Rose is confounded. Her stare becomes a frown. It becomes dismay. "You wish me to befriend a man I do not know? A man I have never met?"

Black still holds up his hand, though it no longer commands. "Father Tenderson will introduce you," he says because he wants to hurry away. "Or Father Whorry."

Then he touches his hat and withdraws into the crowd.

Rose follows the stranger with her eyes until she loses sight of him. She hardly feels Arbor tug at her hand. She hardly hears her daughter ask, "Can we, Ma? Can we meet him? The man who needs us?" The stranger has turned the mother's world on its head, and she is no longer sure of her balance. She is nodding, but she does not know what she will do.

She does not know that Black has already put her from his mind. His thoughts run ahead of him rather than behind, traveling a road to a destination he cannot see, as he sifts through the throng until he clears the square. When he is able to gaze down the street, he scans it for the sign of the inn he seeks.

Soon he locates it. It is where the Dark priest told him it would be. At once, he ascends to the series of porches on that side and strides toward his goal. In his haste, he neglects to touch his hat to the townsfolk. They stare at him harder as he passes.

As he expects in a town of this size, the inn is also a tavern. Its swinging doors admit him to a room both larger and more elaborate than Bailey's establishment. It has chandeliers for light and padded chairs at round tables for its patrons. Long mirrors behind the bar reflect the bustle of serving-maids and boys carrying a greater variety of viands than Bailey can offer. And in its own fashion, the place is as crowded as the square. Father Whorry has advised Black well. A profusion of wines, ales, and spirits flows as wagoneers, caravaners, and their guards demand refreshment after their long deprivation. Half or more of the men and women who have come with the caravan will resume their journey on the morrow with aching heads and complaining stomachs.

Amid the confusion, however, the shouts for service or companionship, the noise of camaraderie, and the clatter of eating, Black identifies the caravan-master without difficulty. She has the arms of a muleteer, the hands of a gravedigger, the hair of a wind-storm, and the bulk of a steer, but it is not by those signs that he knows her. He is sure of her because she sits at the only table that does not strain to accommodate too many patrons. Also her back is to the wall and her face to the door, she drinks sparingly, and the two men she permits to share her table defer to her as they eat.

As Black enters, the caravaners pay no heed, but every gaze that resides in Settle's Crossways snaps to him as though he has come flinging daggers.

Like the inn itself, and its patrons, this does not surprise Black. He expects it, not because he is a stranger, but rather by reason of his actions against Ing Hardiston and the storekeeper's comrades. He judges that Hardiston would not talk about his own defeat willingly, or permit his deeds to reflect discreditably on him. But the storekeeper needed a healer, as did one of his men. An explanation would be required. Therefore he will have told his version of events—a courageous, honorable version—to everyone he encounters. By now, half the town has heard Ing Hardiston's tale.

This does not trouble Black. He has no use for the town's good will. And he sees no indication that Hardiston's tale has reached the caravan-master. She notices his arrival as she notices everything, but she betrays no reaction that will prevent him from speaking to her, or discourage her from answering.

Ignoring the townsfolk, he makes his way among the tables until he stands in front of Kelvera.

When she meets his gaze, he says her name with his accustomed silk. Without asking her permission, without removing his hat and cloak, he seats himself opposite her. She rests her forearms on the table. He does not. Her companions stare at him, openly astonished, but he does not regard them.

"Kelvera," he says again. "Forgive my discourtesy. I must speak with you. The matter is urgent."

He surprises her, though she gives no sign of her reaction. She is experienced and wily. In her many years of long journeys, guiding caravans through lands unknown to all but her and her captains, she has seen much, heard much, learned much. She knows a shaped man when she meets with one. They are rare in this kingdom, and have become more so since the ending of the old wars. Still she is certain that if this man exposes his arms, he will reveal an astonishing variety of glyphs, sigils, scarifications, and inlaid metals.

Holding the stranger's gaze, she tells her companions, "Another table."

They rise from their chairs at once, though they do not mask their reluctance. One is her captain of guards. He commands the defense of her train. He does not pretend equanimity as he draws a poniard from his belt, shows it to the stranger, then stabs it into the table where it is ready for Kelvera's use. The other man is her captain of wagons, responsible for managing the diverse owners, burdens, teamsters, and beasts of her train. More readily than the guard captain, he goes to request a seat at a nearby table.

Black does not acknowledge the captains. Waiting, he ignores the poniard.

The caravan-master leans back in her chair. She does not judge the shaped man or determine her response in advance. Nor does she invite him to share her meal. When she has appraised him for a moment, searching her memories of other travels through this land, she says, "Call me Blossom." Endless days of shouting have made her voice gruff as a grindstone. "You are?"

"Black," he replies without hesitation. He is already sure of her. She will answer him or she will not. If she does, she will do so honestly. If she does not, she will betray no hint of what she withholds.

"Black, hmm?" muses Kelvera. "Interesting." Her tone suggests disinterest. "Not a name I know."

Black shrugs. He does not respond.

The caravan-master studies his silence. With an air of distraction, as though she is unaware of what she does, she reaches out and taps the hilt of her guard captain's poniard. "An urgent matter, you said? Then speak. I cannot guess your mind."

Black nods. "Blossom," he says. Despite his haste, he hopes to distract her from her natural suspicions. "Why are you called Blossom?"

She raises her eyebrows. "*That* is what you wish to know? And you call it urgent? I am Blossom because it pleases me."

Black almost smiles. "And I am Black because I have forgotten my other names. My travels have been as long as yours. I forget what I can. The rest is urgent. If it were not, I would forget it as well."

Kelvera feels a tension in her shoulders easing. Rare as they are, shaped men are dangerous, and this one more so than others. Now, however, she understands that he is not dangerous to her. Frowning, she draws the poniard from the table and pushes it away from her.

"Then speak," she repeats. "Those who trust me to lead them have their secrets. I will keep them. But anything else—" She spreads her hands to indicate the world she knows.

"Have you incurred losses?" he asks abruptly.

She squints at him. "What, *ever*?"

"In this kingdom," he explains. "On this journey."

"No," she answers. Then she admits, "Attacks are inevitable. The wealth of my caravans is legend. But my captain of guards knows his duties. His men are well trained and armed. One guard took a spear in his thigh. An arrow killed the personal servant of a dealer in fine spices. We left seven brigands dead. I do not call the outcome losses."

Black nods again. "And no desertions?"

Kelvera slaps her hand on the table. She pretends indignation. "I treat my people well, men and women. They do not desert." After a moment, she laughs humorlessly. "Not in this kingdom. The old wars began here. They ended here. This land is considered perilous. Shapers and wild powers are said to remain, perhaps hidden in this very forest. Even cowards do not desert here."

Black's manner remains abrupt. "When did you last pass this way?" He means from west to east, from the strange deserts in the far west to the richly mined mountains a hundred leagues eastward.

The question catches Kelvera off guard. She counts backward in her mind. "Two seasons ago? No, more. But less than three."

"Did you incur any losses *then*? Any desertions?" Black needs an explanation for Tamlin Marker's killer's ability to claim so many brigands without the aid of followers known in the town. "Did any wagons leave your train?"

The caravan-master collects her thoughts. "Any wagons?" She dismisses losses and desertions. "In this kingdom? Before the destinations they hired me to reach?"

Any matter that a shaped man considers urgent is important to her as well, though her reasons are not his. If Black is not dangerous to her, his presence and his questions imply danger nonetheless. His interest is a warning she means to heed.

For the third time, Black nods.

"Yes," she replies slowly. She makes certain of her memories. "But not in Settle's Crossways. A league to the east. In virgin forest. Near that misplaced mountain, the old fumer. For no discernible reason."

Soft as feathers on clean skin, Black urges, "Tell me."

"We had not left the desert," she answers, still slowly, "when a wagon purchased a place among us." She trusts him to know of the desert she mentions. "Its owner was an old man. More than old. He appeared ancient, with a face cut by the erosion of years, skin worn thin until it seemed transparent, and a frame much emaciated. He wore a long robe that may once have been red, but was now faded to rust. His beard, white and well-kempt, reached to his waist. Altogether he resembled a hierophant who had given his life to the worship of a desert god."

Black prepares another question, but Kelvera does not pause. Having chosen to answer, she answers fully.

"Still his movements were not decrepit," she continues. "Indeed, his steps were sprightly when he elected to walk, which was seldom. Also his voice was not ancient, though it quavered. At times, laboring caravans raise a mighty din, yet he was able to make himself heard.

"We required a name. He allowed us to call him Sought.

"With him, he brought four guards, and also a teamster for his oxen, but no personal servant. We called his lack of an attendant strange, yet his wagon was stranger. It was all of wood, more a house on wheels than a wagon, and painted the same worn hue as his robe. Also it was made without windows—without as much as chinks between the boards—to ease the heat within. Its only opening was a door at the rear, a door too sturdy to be forced, which remained locked at all times."

The caravan-master shrugs. She has no cause to doubt her choices. "I accepted his company. I did not begrudge him his strangeness, and the price he offered was generous. But I would have accepted him without payment for the sake of his guards.

"My men are good. His surpassed them. I have rarely seen arms and armor of such quality. Their training was diligent, their skill prodigious, and their vigilance in their master's name exceeded all bounds. If they ever ate or slept"—she remembers them with as much awe as her nature allows—"I say this seriously, Black—they did so only when he admitted one or at most two of them to his house. With four such men in my employ, I could dispense with ten others and call myself well defended."

For a moment, Kelvera drifts among her memories. To prompt her, Black asks, "He named his destination, this Sought?"

Her full attention returns to the shaped man. "He did not," she replies more sharply. "He said that he would go with me as far as I went. Then he would find another caravan to continue his journey."

"Yet he turned aside?"

She folds her arms. "As I have said. He did not emerge from his wagon while we rested here. But when we had passed a league beyond Settle's Crossways, his teamster pulled his oxen from the road. There the old man informed my captain of wagons that he was content. He needed rest, he said. He would bide where he was for a time. His guards would suffice to fend for him."

"Fend for him?" Black interjects. The phrase troubles him. It matches his hasty speculations too closely.

Again Kelvera shrugs. "So he said. As he asked no return of coin, I had no cause to refuse him."

Black is silent for a moment. Within himself, he wonders whether his purpose will require him to confront a foe he cannot comprehend. A foe against whom his own powers will have no meaning. Despite his ability to forget, and his singular resolve, he is forced to acknowledge—not for the first time—that he is afraid.

Yet he masks his uncertainty. His manner is unchanged as he asks, "The place where he joined your train. Is it known for its winds?"

"Known?" snorts Kelvera. "Say infamous. It is an unholy hell of winds. Their dust can strip the flesh from bones. Every outcropping of rock has been sculpted until it resembles a fiend yearning for release. Those winds—" She shakes her head to dispel thoughts of over-turned wagons, mangled deaths, spilled goods, maimed beasts. "There is a price in pain to be paid for crossing that stretch of desert."

By these words, Kelvera tells Black that the land of her birth holds to an alien theology, one which would not be recognized in the kingdom he serves. The temples created by the King have not yet excreted such arcana as hells and fiends. Perhaps sorceries are possible in the west that are inconceivable here.

———

He knows now that he has entered deep waters. For him, they may be bottomless. Nevertheless his purpose is at its most compulsory when he fears it.

As he gathers himself to thank the caravan-master, however, his doubts prompt one more question.

"A dire desert, then," he remarks. "What gods are worshipped there?"

If the old man is in truth a hierophant—

Kelvera rolls her eyes. "What else?" She has her own reasons to scorn religions. "Wind and sun. In that region, there are no other powers that can be asked for mercy." Then she shrugs once more. "Those prayers are not answered."

Thinking, Lungs and livers, air and heat, Black can delay no longer. He must obey his purpose.

But when he rises from his chair, the caravan-master stops him with a gesture. He has warned her. She has a warning of her own to deliver.

Leaning close, she says, "Heed me, Black," a whisper no one will overhear. "You are a shaped man. That Sought was not. Be wary of him."

Black raises an eyebrow at her recognition. She does not need to say the words he hears. If the old man is not shaped, he may yet be a shaper. Also his guards are fearsome.

More formally than is his custom, Black replies, "Accept my gratitude, Blossom. I am in your debt."

This debt he hopes to repay.

Kelvera returns a smile as disturbing as his. The more she

thinks on him, the more she desires to understand the danger. It may spill onto her caravan. "Perhaps," she suggests, "we will meet again."

She means to add, When we do, we can discuss who is in debt. But Black forestalls her. He is in haste. "We will not," he says like a man who is already gone. Giving her no time to respond, he strides for the doors.

Still he wants guidance. It will shorten his search. At the doors, he pauses to grip the arm of the most recent arrival, a burly chandler still wearing his leather apron mottled with dried wax. Black invokes his sigil of command as he demands the location of Haul Varder's workshop.

The chandler glowers, torn between umbrage, distorted rumors, and an inability to refuse. He tries to sound angry as he directs Black. To some extent, he succeeds.

At once, Black releases the man. Through the swinging doors, he leaves the inn and enters the glare of the midafternoon sun.

He is at his most certain when he is afraid.

⁓

Two streets and three alleys from the inn, he finds the wheel-wright's smithy and woodshop. The structure resembles an open-sided barn, providing abundant space for Haul Varder's forge at one end and his lathes at the other. Near the forge stands an anvil. Between and above the ends, he has storage for his iron and hammers, for his supplies of wood, and for racks to hold his chisels, saws, and other tools.

The place is near the edge of the town. But this stretch of Settle's Crossways is not extensive. Black judges that he is two hundred paces from Jon Marker's house, perhaps three hundred from the caravan's road. Above the workshop's roof to the east, he can see the tops of the nearest trees.

He hopes to find his quarry there, but he is not surprised when he does not. If the ritual that required Tamlin Marker's murder is near its culmination—and if the wheelwright is involved, as Black now believes—the final preparations are being made. And they are certainly not being made in the town. They are not being made anywhere that risks witnesses. Their perpetrators will seek seclusion against even the most obscure mischance.

The ashes in the forge are cold. They have been cold for some time. The sawdust around the lathes has not been swept. The lathes themselves wear a fine fur of dust, as do their tools. If Black had spent more time questioning townsfolk, he would no doubt have learned how long the shop has been unattended. But he does not need that knowledge. The scent of evil is strong here, as acrid as acid, as bitter as kale, and fraught with intimations of bloodshed. To his shaped senses, it is as distinct as murder, overriding even the stink of cold ashes and the warm odor of drying resins. He will be able to follow it.

A brief stroking of his thigh summons his horse. While he

waits, he searches for some sign of Haul Varder's intent, some indication left by carelessness or haste. But the search does not have his full attention. Kelvera has answered his more practical questions. It is his need for understanding that troubles him. He cannot gauge the peril ahead of him. He is forced to consider that an impossible ritual may be the only possible explanation for the smell that haunts his nose.

His mount greets him with a soft whicker as it trots forward. Despite the hard use he made of it earlier, it is strong and ready, as refreshed as a horse that has enjoyed days of rest and rich pasturage. The ways that it has been shaped are subtle, difficult to discern, but they are potent. The beast will not fail him until he fails himself.

He checks his horse's girth and tack, an old habit. Then he mounts. Though he is no longer patient and believes that he knows his way, he circles the workshop twice, testing the air in every direction. When he is done, he trots toward the eastern outskirts of the town.

There near the fringe of the forest, Settle's Crossways is a haphazard collection of buildings. The shifting sunlight shows him several large warehouses belonging, no doubt, to prosperous merchants. It shows him hovels where the town's poor scrabble for shelter, hoping that their proximity to the warehouses will ease their efforts to find work. And among the hovels and warehouses, he discovers a scattering of more sturdy homes. These lack such amenities as roofed porches. Their owners are not reluctant to enter with mud, dirt, and the droppings of horses and cattle on their boots. Still they are solid houses, made to last. They belong to men or families who do not care for appearances, but who mean to be secure in their homes.

Black does not expect to see lights in the windows at this time of day. They face the westering sun. Their occupants do not yet need lamps. But the windows of one house glow. Covered as they are with oiled cloths, they give him no glimpse of what waits inside. With the sun on them, they should not glow as they do. Yet they are unmistakable in the dwindling afternoon.

The scent of evil leads Black to the lit house.

He dismounts. Silent as nightfall, he approaches the door. When he places his palm there, he knows at once that his quarry is absent. This is Haul Varder's house. The odor of his doings permeates the door, the walls, the glowing windows. Black is sure. But the wheelwright is not here.

Someone else occupies the house. Someone else lights lamps against the coming darkness. That someone, alone, has lit a profusion of lamps.

Black considers departing as he came, in silence. He can follow the obscenity of Tamlin Marker's murder unaided. He does not fear the men who killed the brigands. But an impulse overtakes him, and he knocks.

The quaver of an old voice calls, "What?" An old woman's voice. "Go away. He is not here. Leave me to my prayers."

Black does not ask permission to enter. Lifting the latch, he steps into a room lit by a noonday sun of lamps, lanterns, and candles.

The old woman sits in a comfortless wooden chair surrounded by many lights. Her hearth is cold, but she does not need its warmth. The flames give abundant heat. A dew of sweat glistens on her brow and gathers in the seams of her face, giving her the look of a woman who has labored too long in the last years of her life. Nevertheless she wears a heavy shawl over her shoulders, and she clutches it to her breast as though she imagines that it will protect her.

She turns her head unerringly toward Black, and he sees at once that she is blind. The milky hue that covers her eyes is too thick to permit sight. Still she has heard him. She knows where he stands, just as she knows every lamp, lantern, and taper around her. She keeps them lit at every hour of the day and night. When one or several go out, she refills or replaces them with no fear that she will set herself or the house aflame. It is not Haul Varder who desires them, though the woman does not need them. They are her prayers.

"You dare?" she croaks at Black. She sounds both querulous and frightened. "Be gone. Leave me. When he catches you, he will teach you to respect his mother."

"I do not fear him," Black replies like the coming night. "You have no cause to fear me. Only tell me what he does, and I will go. Only tell me where he is, and I will go."

"*Tell?*" the old woman retorts. The puckering of her mouth betrays her toothless gums. "*I?* Tell *you*? I will tell you nothing. You are a blackguard who preys on weakness. I am a gods-fearing woman, gods-fearing. I do not go to the temples. I cannot walk so far. But that does not make me evil. I worship *here*, do you understand? I worship *here*. There is no temple-goer more devout.

"If you do not go—if he does not catch you—I will call down Bright Eternal's light to consume you. I will cast you into Dark Enduring's agony."

To an extent, Black believes her. He does not doubt that she will hurl her lamps and lanterns at him, as many as she can reach. He does not doubt that her aim will be good. But he also knows that he will not burn. His cloak and his shaping will ward him. Still he seeks to calm her. If she acts against him, her house will become conflagration. He will be forced to rescue her. He may be forced to find aid for her before he can resume his purpose.

In his mildest tone, his softest silk, he asks, "Who speaks of evil? I did not."

"Blackguard," she snaps. As her fright fades, her bitterness grows. "Do you think to confuse me? I know you. You are the canker that rots the heart of this town. You do not speak of evil *now*. You are too cunning for that. But you did *then*. You were not so bold to say it to my face, but you said it. You said it behind it my back, a gods-fearing woman's back. You said it and did not admit your wrong. You did not ask my forgiveness."

Sweat gathers on her brow. It trickles into her eyes. But she does not blink it away. It is not sorrow or regret. It is an old woman's trembling fury.

"If you had said it to my face, I would have told you that I see as clearly as you, indeed I do. And I have a clearer sight of my duty. There *was* evil in him then. He was a wicked boy, cursed son of a cursed father. Did you think me blind to it? But there is no evil *now*. With my own love and my own strength, I ripped it from his heart after his father forsook us. With punishment and prayer, I drove it out. *Out*, do you hear me? I scarred him with my love until he had no room in him for evil.

"He is a good man *now*." She smacks her lips in satisfaction, but does not ease her clutch on her shawl. "A good neighbor with a good living. A kind man who aids the less fortunate. A hard-working man who provides for his gods-fearing mother, his lonely mother, his blind mother. He cares for her with the diligence of a priest.

"When he catches you, he will drive you from the house. He will drive you to your ruin. When he is done with you, you will beg me on your *knees* for forgiveness"—quavering, she summons the fullness of her anger—"*and I will not give it.*"

Black has heard enough. Such men as Haul Varder do not spring from the earth. They are shaped much as Black himself has been shaped, though by different means. If his purpose and his circumstances permit it, Black will take pity on Haul Varder, for surely the wheelwright's mother did not.

Tracing a pattern across his chest with one hand, Black grips the edge of his cloak with the other. "He will not catch me," he assures the old woman. "I will catch *him*."

Then he swings his cloak in a sweeping gesture that extinguishes every light in the house. When the woman begins to wail, he turns his back on her, strides outside, and leaps for his horse. At a gallop, he rides in pursuit of his quarry.

～❦～

He cannot gallop when he enters the forest. The trees are thick, and the day's light becomes dusk quickly among them. If he turns aside until he comes to the road, he will make better haste. Nonetheless he stays within the woods, following the scent of Haul Varder's crimes. He is on a track the wheelwright has taken many times. It will lead him to his destination. Trusting his horse to give him as much speed as it can, he sharpens his senses so that errant breezes or undiscovered corpses will not urge him astray.

He expects an ambush. He knows nothing of the old man who calls himself Sought. He knows only what Kelvera has told him of the man's bodyguards. It is possible that they are ignorant of him. They have come from a land far to the west, where the King's mediation does not hold sway. Their ignorance may be complete. Yet Black thinks otherwise. He will be surprised if Haul Varder has not been in Settle's Crossways during the past night and day. He considers it unlikely that the wheelwright has not heard gossip of the stranger who spoke with Trait in the tavern, the stranger who injured Ing Hardiston and another man at Tamlin Marker's grave. He believes that Sought's men will be ready for him.

The sun's setting behind him casts spots like fragments of Varder's mother's prayers through the boughs and leaves, spots that dance and waver in the low wind, obscuring more than they reveal. Each instance of brightness darkens what lies behind it. But Black does not regard them. He has other senses, forms of perception that are not misled by the sun's last fireflies. He trusts what he is able to discern. All other concerns he puts from his mind. That he does not, can not, understand the purpose that drives his quarry dismays him, but it does not affect his resolve, or his haste, or his confidence in his mount. It does not make him less the servant of his own purpose.

Lungs and livers, air and heat. And a hierophant from a land infamous for its winds, a land where wind and sun are worshipped as gods. If it is true that air and heat are elemental spirits, as necessary to life as bright and dark, it may also be true that a shaper born to a parched and baking world knows how to call upon gods that have played no part in Black's homeland's wars.

The ability to make use of such knowledge here is incomprehensible to Black, but his lack of understanding does not make it impossible.

His mount stretches to leap a fallen tree. It skitters aside from a thicket of longthorn briar, avoids a sinkhole in a wandering stream, picks a careful path between large boulders. Its care makes him a target for his attackers.

He is aware of them while they still only hear his approach. He counts four men armed with sabers and other weapons. He recognizes their stealth. He knows that the wheelwright is not among them.

He detects a crossbow aimed at his hip from the brush on one side, a spear poised to throw from the shelter of an old oak on the other. A man with a dagger ready crouches to spring from atop the nearest boulder. Directly ahead of Black, ten or more paces distant, stands a fourth assailant, waiting with his quarter-staff in case Black is able to evade three simultaneous assaults.

Black's movements are mapped in his mind, as precise as though he has foreseen them. Snatching up the edge of his cloak, he catches the bolt of the crossbow in the tough canvas as he vaults from the far side of his horse. The spear plucks at his shoulder, but does not harm him. The man leaping from the boulder lands in the mount's empty saddle.

An instant of surprise slows Black's attackers, an instant of harsh cursing. During that heartbeat's pause, Black slaps his horse's rump, causing the beast to buck the man from its back. Prompt to its training, its shaping, the horse begins to trample the fallen man.

Two or three paces of ground are now clear in front of Black. As one assailant bursts from the brush and another charges past his oak, both drawing their sabers, Black invokes his longsword. Kelvera has warned him against the skill of Sought's men. As he engages them, he sees that she did not exaggerate. His own skill suffices against one such opponent. Only the many ways in which he has been shaped enable him to counter two.

Parrying with his utmost speed, he shifts his ground until he has a boulder at his back. With both men in front of him, he fights for his life.

Thrust and parry, slash and counter, his blade and theirs weave a skein of imminent bloodshed through the gloom. The last glints of the sun strike sparks like stars on the swift iron, gleams briefer than blinks. Black's horse has fled among the trees. The beast has left one of Sought's bodyguards broken or dead. There is much to be said for killing both of his immediate attackers, and also the last, who still waits. He imagines that Sought relies on them. Their deaths may prevent the culmination of the ritual that claimed Tamlin Marker. But he cannot be certain of this. Perhaps Haul Varder is all the aid Sought needs. Also he is not confident that he *can* kill his opponents. They are indeed exceptional. And they do not tire, though he resists them with all the strength of his body, all the gifts of his shaping, all the experience of his many battles. If he grants one of his foes an opening, he may be able to cut down the other. But then he will be wounded himself. Killing them both is not a likely outcome.

Without hesitation, almost without thought, he changes his tactics. He fights now, not to harm or drive back his attackers, but rather to make himself a different target. He means to cause them to adjust their footing. And when he sees a subtle alteration in how they balance themselves, he takes his chance.

Headlong, he dives between them, hoping that their blades will not find his back as he passes.

They are wrongly balanced to turn and strike while he is exposed. For the merest instant, they interfere with each other. Neither man can swing without hazard to his comrade.

Black's dive becomes a roll. He surges to his feet facing the foes he has passed. In the same motion, he springs to assail them.

He understands what will happen now. He recognizes it as it occurs. The last bodyguard is charging. Black feels the blow of the quarterstaff coming. He knows how to evade it, but he does not do so. Instead he accepts it. When it strikes the back of his head, he accepts the shock, the blinding pain, the fall into unconsciousness.

The blow will not kill him. He is too hardy. But it will take him where he needs and fears to go.

～

When he returns to himself, he is bound spread-eagled by his wrists and ankles. At first, he knows only that he cannot move. Then the pain finds him. The agony in his head is like that of a spear driven through his skull. The back of his head is a sodden mess. Blood drips down his neck to his shoulders. Waves of nausea and the bright echoes of the blow that took him make his guts squirm. They prevent him from opening his eyes. Of his circumstances, he knows only that he is helpless.

His wound is not mortal. It is worse than mortal. It has made him a victim.

The heat is tremendous. It seems to scald his skin. It has probably burned away his eyebrows and lashes. The hair on his head may be gone. When he tries to blink, his lids scrape his eyes.

Nevertheless the ways in which he has been shaped go deep. His bleeding slows. With every breath, his nausea eases. Gradually tears moisten his eyes. In stabbing surges, the pain of his head spreads through him. It restores sensation to his limbs. He finds that he is able to close his fingers. He can move his toes.

Now he feels the pressure of rope on his wrists and ankles. It is woven of sisal or some other harsh fiber. It will not break. And it allows no more than a slight flexing of his elbows and knees. He can bend his joints to achieve subtle shifts of his posture. He cannot gain leverage.

He is not ready to see where he is. But the rough touch of the surface at his back tells him that he is pinned against native rock. It is crude, studded with protrusions and gaps, written with ridges. He can imagine that he is bound to a boulder, but he believes that he is not. He believes that he is fixed to a wall. The fierce heat and its brimstone reek convince him that he is in a cavern.

Though his eyes are closed, he knows that the space is filled with ruddy light.

From some distant source comes a low sound like the slow boiling of a cauldron.

Then the life returning to his nerves makes him aware that his plight is worse than helplessness. The heat on his skin tells him that he is naked. More than his cloak and hat have been taken from him. All of his garments have been stripped away. Even his boots are gone. Even the bindings of his loins—

He is exposed for what he is. Every detail of his shaping is visible, every detail except those on his back. From neck to foot, the elaborate sweeps and whorls of his scarification are revealed. They speak a language known to every shaper in the kingdom. The deeply tattooed sigils name and define him. The burned glyphs invoke the powers imminent in his scars. The thin bars of purest silver inlaid under his skin summon the energies of bright and dark to enhance his senses, his strength, his resolve. Together, the inlays, his glyphs and sigils, and his scarifications bind him to his purpose.

If he hoped now, which he does not, he would hope that Haul Varder's ignorance of shaping, and Sought's presumed ignorance of how bright and dark are called upon, will protect him from a complete betrayal of the King. If Sought's learning suffices to interpret what he sees—to interpret all he sees—Black's body will tell him how the King's mediation can be foiled.

Black has found that he is able to close his fingers. Now he clenches his fists firmly. He means to conceal what little he can.

When he begins to distinguish voices from the sound of distant boiling, he opens his eyes and blinks them clear.

He is bound to the wall of a cavern the size of the square where roads intersect in Settle's Crossways. The ropes at his wrists and ankles are tied to iron stakes pounded into the rough stone. Much of the floor in front of him is level until it is cut off by a rift or crevice that extends the width of the cavern. This fissure is the source of the reddish light and the terrible heat. It is also the source of the boiling. Clearly it goes far down into the heart of the rock.

From the rift arises a thick, acrid fume, but it does not fill the cavern. Around the walls are a number of natural tunnels, and the cavern's ceiling has the shape of a funnel. Drawing air from the tunnels, the hot fume streams upward and away until it emerges from the throat of the mountain, the old fumer in the east.

The air from the tunnels is all that prevents the heat from destroying Black and his captors.

Off to one side stands a wagon that resembles a house on wheels. Its only door is open, but Black cannot see inside.

With him in the cavern are four men. Three he recognizes by their arms and armor, by the way they move. They are the guards he fought in the forest. The fourth is surely Haul Varder. He has neither weapons nor protection. He is naked to the waist in the heat, and his chest weeps sweat. He has a black beard like a glower, the muscles of a blacksmith, the solid frame of a laborer. His hands are so heavily callused that he cannot close them completely. Of the four, only he watches the wagon. Only he is impatient. In his eyes, the ruddy light burns like excitement or fear.

The three guards keep watch on Black, but they betray no particular interest in him, no animosity for the death of their comrade. Black's helplessness contents them. They will react to him only if he struggles, and then only if his struggles threaten to free him.

Sweltering, Haul Varder paces the stone. He has been promised much, and has done much to fulfill his role in Sought's ritual. He has in him a wellspring of cold rage that has enabled him to commit deeds he would not have imagined without the old man's promises. At Father Whorry's urging, and because Sought wished it, he accepted Jon Marker as his shop servant. Grinding his teeth, he endured Jon Marker's insufferable courtesy and meekness and labor, though he knew the man's demeanor was false. He knows too well that all courtesy and meekness are false, feigned by men who seek to conceal their contempt, men who know him and his mother and hold only scorn. Still he did as he was bid. Because he had dealings with men who had dealings with robbers and cutthroats, he could guide the old man's guards to the camps of brigands. With his own hands, he took insufferable Jon Marker's insufferable son. With the old man's guidance, he harvested the boy's lungs and liver while the boy still lived. In every way, he has served Sought's commands and whims, and has endured the old man's disdain. He desires what he has been promised more than he craves respect. For him, all respect is false. He will never trust in it.

No, Haul Varder does not wish for respect. He covets fear. It is his dream, and the old man's promise, that he will be feared. That he will be feared so extremely that strong men will loose their bowels and women will grovel in the dirt.

———

He is impatient to see the old man's promise honored.

Vexed and suffering in the heat, the wheelwright waits as long as he can. Then he shouts at the wheeled house, "Enough! It is *enough*! I have endured too much of your preparations and researches. Is there no end to your dithering? When will you let me kill him?"

He believes that Black's death will transform him. It will make him fearsome.

"*Kill* him?" the old man answers. In normal tones, his voice is a quaver that masks its strength. Now it is a shriek. "Imbecile! We *do not* kill him!"

In a fury of haste, Sought leaves his dwelling. He springs to the stone with the lithe confidence of a much younger man, a newer priest. His beard spills aside in the breezes from the various tunnels. He wears a long robe colored or dulled to the same hue as the light from the fissure. It is voluminous and flutters about him, giving the impression that inside it he has spent decades in near-starvation. Its secret is that it conceals many pockets containing various powders and implements, some or all of which may be needed at any moment.

The stiff mass of his eyebrows gives him a look of perpetual astonishment, yet he is not surprised by Haul Varder's presumption. He is only surprised at himself. Immersed in his last preparations, in the near fruition of his life's work, he forgets too easily that lesser men are sheep-headed fools. It is only the near-mindless fidelity of his guards that allows him to stand so close to the achievement of pure glory.

Exalted by the heat, Sought sweeps forward. Clutching the wheelwright's sweat-slick arm, he drags the man closer to Black. An arm's length away, he halts. "We do *not* kill him," he repeats, openly exasperated. "Are you blind? Look!"

He points to the sigil on Black's right shoulder. "There." He indicates a glyph decorated with scars on Black's ribs. "There." He directs Haul Varder's gaze to an extravagant whorl in the flesh of Black's lower abdomen. "*There.*

"The signs are plain. This man is the King's Justice. We are indeed fortunate that he has come against us. I will make good use of his enhancements. Yet for that very reason, he must live. If he is slain, the King will know it. Even at this distance, he will attempt to intervene.

"You do not understand the danger. I have spent an age of my life in study, and lakes of blood as well. Still I cannot measure the reach of the King's powers. I know only that they are great. To end the wars as he did, they must be great indeed. We will not risk his awareness of what we do."

Then Sought shrugs. He releases Haul Varder. Swallowing his ire, he says, "When we are done, we will not care who knows. The King can feel as much fear as any man. Until then, his Justice will serve us. We will take his inlays"—he muses for a moment—"perhaps two or three of his glyphs"—then he continues more strongly—"and as much blood as he can spare. But we will not allow him to breathe his last until our task is complete."

None of this surprises Black. He knows there is sorcery in his blood, a necessary effect of his shaping. He knows Sought can take power from his veins as well as from his silver, and from other details also. And he finds that he now understands more than he imagined. The conundrum that has baffled him since he heard Jon Marker and studied Tamlin Marker's grave is the impossibility of concentrating the elemental energies of heat and air so that they will serve as a source of power. But here that riddle is answered. The slow boil of stone in the crevice will supply Sought with all the concentration he can require.

Then there will arise a form of sorcery for which the King is unprepared. No amount of resolve and strength will suffice to preserve the balance to which the King has given his life.

His fists Black keeps closed. Perhaps Sought has not studied them. Perhaps the hierophant does not know that there is thin silver under the surface of Black's palms.

Haul Varder does not understand Sought's caution. He does not care to understand it. Explanations and warnings only aggravate his impatience. He is entirely aware of the old man's scorn. He does not trust Sought to fulfill any promise. Yet if there is doubt in the wheelwright's eyes, if there is fear, he does not know it. His rage overcomes every qualm, every scruple, every hesitation.

"Then do it," he demands. "Cut him. Take what you need. Keep your word. I am done with your endless preparations. They are *timid*, old man. They show that you are unsure of yourself.

"He is helpless now. He will not be more helpless in an hour's time."

Sought replies with a smile like a wolf's. The wheelwright's insults stoke his own hot hungers, but he does not speak of them. Instead he offers his mildest quaver.

"Very well. I am ready. At your request, we will begin."

Holding Haul Varder's gaze, the hierophant nods to his guards.

They have been well instructed. They know their master's will. It rules them. One remains with Sought and Haul Varder. His comrades cross the cavern to enter the wagon.

When they emerge, they are carrying two square-cut timbers, one twice the length of the other. They have rope. Near Black, they lean the longer timber against the wall. With rope, they lash the shorter timber across the longer. When they are done, they have fashioned a rude cross.

Haul Varder snorts at the sight. "What purpose does *that* serve?" The wellspring of his rage provides an abundance of bitterness. "Is this some trick? He cannot be made more helpless than he is. I can do whatever I wish to him as he stands."

Black has a better understanding of the old man's intent. Any ritual of shaping must begin with natural flesh. He is not surprised when the guard at Sought's side strikes the wheelwright's head, a clout that drops him to the stone. While Haul Varder writhes in pain and shock, stunned by the blow, Sought's servants drag him to the cross. With practiced ease, they bind his arms to the shorter timber. His ankles they secure near the floor. When they are done, Tamlin Marker's killer is as helpless as Black.

The guards do not remove Haul Varder's trousers. Sought has seen Black's legs. He has studied them. He knows that their shaping contributes much to Black's purpose, but will not serve his own.

As the wheelwright recovers, he shakes his head frantically. "This is not—" His voice fails him until the effects of the blow diminish. Then he is able to shout. "This is not your promise! Bastard! Whoreson! I did not consent to *this*! You assured me I did my part when I killed the boy. When I harvested him." His eyes glare in his head like a madman's. "*This is not your promise!*"

Sought now stands in front of Black. He is planning his cuts, his maimings. He does not disguise his eagerness as he answers Haul Varder.

"You did your part. Indeed, you did. I acknowledge it freely. And I will fulfill my promise. You will see how I fulfill it. But the boy's death required your willingness. For my ritual, innocence must be voluntarily taken. If one of my men did the deed for me, the effect of the outcome would be lessened.

"Now I do not need your willingness. It has no further use. For the fulfillment of my promise, you are merely an implement. By choice or not, you suffice."

Haul Varder screams his rage and fear, but Sought no longer heeds him. The gaze with which the priest regards Black suggests that the old man is amazed to come so near his goal, but Sought knows only his own eagerness. After so many years of toil, so many victims, so much extreme deprivation, so much arcane study, he now stands in the perfect place for his purpose, and has been given the perfect tools to achieve his ends. No hierophant has ever accomplished what he attempts here. He finds that he must take a moment to calm himself so that his hands will not tremble.

From hidden pockets, he draws out a delicate knife of aching keenness and a small vessel shaped like a trough slightly curved. Pressing the vessel to Black's flesh, he sets his blade to an inlay below Black's collarbone. With extreme care, he cuts to remove the silver. Black's blood he collects in his vessel.

This is a pain with which Black has long and extensive experience. He accepted it during his shaping. He does not accept it now. Howling hoarsely, he twists as much as he can from side to side, playing the part of a man who squirms in a wasted effort to escape excruciation. Yet his demonstrated agony is a charade. He uses it to disguise the way he invokes the inlays of his palms, the way he strains to free his right arm from its bonds. He knows that he will not break the rope. He has never had such strength. Yet with time and effort, a bolt hammered into stone may be worked loose.

If Sought and the guards do not recognize what he strives to do—

From the place where the bolt enters the wall comes a small sifting of grit, nothing more.

With one thin bar of silver removed, the old man sets his vessel aside. He confronts Haul Varder. Vexed by the wheelwright's screams and curses, Sought gestures to his guards. One man steps forward to gag Haul Varder's mouth. The gag is driven so deep that Varder retches. He can scarcely breathe. He cannot scream, though his gaze is white terror.

Satisfied, Sought finds a place among Haul Varder's ribs, a place unlike the inlay's location in Black's chest. He opens a substantial flap of Varder's skin, inserts the silver, then settles the flap over it. Responding to Sought's nod, another guard uses a leather-hook and twine to sew shut the wound so that the inlay will not shift.

As his servant treats the wheelwright, Sought returns to Black.

Briefly the hierophant considers his task. When he has made his choice, he slashes with his knife again and again at Black's sigil of command, taking care only to catch Black's blood in his vessel. He does not stop until the sigil is marred beyond use or name. Then he proceeds to remove another inlay from Black's chest.

During these cuts, Black continues his raw-throated howls, his twisting, his show of anguish. The slight flexing of his elbow allowed by his bonds does not enable him to exert much force, but he does what he can. And he does not only pull. He jerks upward, downward.

The drift of grit from the place where the bolt enters the stone is not enough.

When the second of Black's inlays has been imposed on Haul Varder, this time deep in the man's belly, and the wound has been sewn shut, Sought begins to draw cuts on the wheelwright's flesh. Some are symbols and whorls that Black recognizes. Others form patterns unfamiliar to him. Soon Haul Varder's torso is a sheen of sweat and blood, his beard is a mute cry for help, and his eyes flutter on the edge of unconsciousness.

For the moment, the old man is content with his work. A sign to his guards brings one of them to remove the gag from Haul Varder's mouth. While the wheelwright whoops for air, Sought retrieves his supply of Black's blood. Obeying a silent command, the guard grips Haul Varder's head and tilts it back. The guard's fingers gouge Varder's nerves until Varder's mouth is forced open.

The old man pours Black's blood down his ally's throat until it has all been swallowed.

Black feels that he is suffocating in the heat. Sweat runs from his body. His new wounds pump trickles of blood. But he ignores those sensations. While Sought's attention, and that of his guards, is occupied with the wheelwright, Black works against the bolt that secures his right hand.

He cannot work long. The hierophant soon returns to him. Sought has much to do to complete his designs. Black endures as best he can, feigning torment, while another of his sigils is destroyed and two more inlays are cut out. As best he can, he fights the bolt. Yet despite his straits, his growing weakness, his imminent betrayal of the King, he finds comfort in Sought's actions. The old man has not touched the signs he indicated to Haul Varder, the signs that demand the King's attention. He avoids attracting the King's notice. Also Sought has not harmed the place on Black's hip that summons his longsword. The priest believes that Black cannot move his arms. Therefore Black cannot invoke his powers. Sought has not examined Black's palms.

The hierophant's knowledge is not as complete as Black feared.

Haul Varder is unconscious now, or he has fallen into the compliance taught by his mother's harsh love. He does not struggle as he is wounded with Black's inlays and the wounds are sewn. He does not protest as Sought's cuts proliferate on his chest and belly, his arms and shoulders. He does not resist drinking Black's blood.

While the wheelwright is shaped, Black risks more obvious efforts to loosen the bolt. He knows that he has little time. Sought's ritual approaches its culmination.

Still the grit falling from the bolt is not enough.

For the first time, Black hears Sought speak to his men. "I must pause," he says. With studious care, he mops blood and sweat from Haul Varder's torso. "One more inlay will be enough. More than enough. But the last cuts are crucial. I must see clearly what I do, and I am old.

"Ready the organs while I rest. Scatter the powders I have prepared on them. Say the words I have taught you. Then bring our harvest out. There must be no delay at the end."

Two guards enter the wagon. They do not return quickly. When they do return, they carry between them a large wooden tub crusted with old blood.

The organs, Black thinks, straining his right arm until the muscles and sinews threaten to tear. The lungs and livers. To invoke heat and air. To rule them. Not the fierce heat from the crevice. Not the comparative cool of breezes from the tunnels. Rather the elemental energies themselves, the gods of heat and air. Concentrated here as they are nowhere else in the kingdom, or in the known lands.

Still Black does not believe that Sought can draw force from air. The hierophant needs lungs only to stoke the fire in the rift, to fan the flames like a bellows. His ritual will evoke the sorcery of heat.

When the old man stands before him again, Black summons his last desperation.

Another inlay Sought cuts out of Black, this one from Black's lower abdomen near his groin. Playing his charade, Black stretches against his bonds like a man on the rack. But he does not exert his full strength. He allows his growing weakness, the effect of his losses, to affect him. When this silver is gone, and his blood has been collected, he slumps in the posture of a man defeated.

He waits until Sought has returned to Haul Varder, until the wheelwright is being cut, until the old man's eagerness and the attention of the guards regard only the ruined man. Then Black puts all that remains of him into his right arm and *pulls*. He pulls until his heart threatens to burst.

Grit trickles from the hole made by the bolt. The bolt wobbles. For an instant, its resistance is greater than Black can endure. Then a cruel effort draws the iron from the stone.

His arm is free.

He is close to fainting, but he does not hesitate. One guard notices his success. Sought himself notices. They will act. One two three, Black slaps the places on his marred body that demand the King's awareness. And with his summons, he sends a piece of his soul. He cannot do otherwise. It is his soul that the King will hear, his soul that the King will understand.

By so doing, Black commits himself to death. Even a shaped man cannot live long when so much of his soul is gone.

Still he regrets nothing. He is near the end of all fear.

And he does not falter in his purpose. A guard rushes toward him. Sought turns in surprise and outrage. Black responds as swiftly as his failing strength allows. He claps his hand to the glyph on his hip that manifests his longsword. With the hilt in his grasp, he swings outward. The tip of his blade catches the guard's throat, but Black does not pause to observe the effect of his slash. His return stroke hacks at the rope binding his left hand to its bolt.

The rope is tough. Though it is damaged, it does not part.

The old man is shaken to the core of his ambitions, his hungers. He knows what Black has done. He knows his peril. But he also does not hesitate. He has come too far for too long to draw back. He snarls an instant's incantation. With one trembling hand, he sketches an arcane symbol across the air.

Black's longsword becomes smoke in his hand. It dissipates quickly, tugged away by the breezes from the tunnels.

The guard is on the floor. He clutches at his neck. Blood

gasps from the severing of his windpipe. Already he is too weak to seek help from his master. In moments, he is dead.

Two servants remain to the old man. They await his bidding.

"Curse you!" Sought yells at Black. He is incandescent with rage. "Curse you to all the hells that were, or are, or will be! Curse you eternally!"

Black replies with a smile that does not encourage confidence. He has taken the hierophant's measure now. He knows that Sought's knowledge is incomplete. He knows the ways in which that knowledge is incomplete. And he knows that the old man's hungers will overcome both his outrage and his danger.

Also Black knows that his own task is not done. His purpose demands more of him.

Writhing in his robe, Sought masters himself. He has only one hope left, and his craving for it is endless. He turns away from Black. To his remaining men, he shouts, "The organs first! *Quickly!* We must complete the ritual before the King can intervene!"

The guards do not delay. They have no personal fears. Despite their great skill with weapons, they are Sought's puppets. As one, they turn to the tub of lungs and livers. Carrying it to the crevice, they heave it and its contents into the depths.

A roaring from the fissure answers them. Black hears louder boiling. He sees flames at the lip of the rift.

"*Now the wheelwright!*" shrieks the old man. "Let him see how I keep my word!"

The guards obey. Returning to the wall, they lift the cross between them. Haul Varder attempts some weak protest, but he is not heeded. Carrying him bound to his crucifixion, Sought's servants approach the fissure. Without ceremony, they drop their victim into the seething heat, the flagrant light.

The roar in the rift resembles the priest's eagerness. It resembles his hunger. A gyre of flame rises into the cavern, circling itself until it is sucked into the funnel of the ceiling.

"Now!" Sought exults to Black. "Gaze on what I have wrought! Gaze and know despair!"

His men stand as though they have forgotten themselves. One or both of them can kill Black now, but they do not move. They have come to the end of their instructions. They wait for their master's commands.

Black does not know what preparations the hierophant has performed in secret. Like the guards, he waits.

The roar has a voice. Black almost understands it, but its meaning is confused in the fissure, in the deep boiling, in the tremendous increase of heat.

A hand of fiery stone grips the rim of the crevice. A shape of flame climbs into view. Black sees a head that may once have been lava. He sees shoulders as heavy as boulders, yet as liquid as molten wax. A second hand grasps the rim. It melts purchase for its fingers in the rock.

Loud in ecstasy or agony, the outcome of Sought's promise to Haul Varder heaves upward. A knee that mars what it touches braces itself on the floor. The voice howls, *"At last!"* Another heave brings the old man's creation to its feet at the edge of the rift. *"Now I am made FEARSOME! I am fear INCARNATE.*

"She will not hurt me again!"

Haul Varder has become lava, or the lava has become him. He retains the shape of a man, though he is twice Black's size. His eyes are the blaze in the heart of a forge. His voice is living heat, and his hands are formed to incinerate lives. His proximity alone turns flesh to tinder. Standing where they have been left to wait, Sought's last servants burn like fagots.

He is Sought's triumph, and his own. No human force can stand against him. He will make infernos of towns and forests. He will burn entire lands to ash. He is ready to rampage wherever he chooses.

For a moment, the old man regards what he has achieved, exulting in his own greatness, and in his creation's. He has proven himself. He has done what no man before has or can. At another time, he would be content. Now, however, seeing the fruition of his life, he wants more. He wants to prove himself against the King.

Then Haul Varder's heat drives Sought back. And when he turns away, he perceives that the crisis of his ambitions has found him. Black and Haul Varder and the smoldering corpses of the guards are not alone.

From the tunnels on one side of the cavern, darkness pours inward. It flows like water over the stone. It is colder than the oldest ice, deeper than the gulfs between the stars. Though it only flows, and does not seek or act, its presence spares Black the worst of the wheelwright's fire. When it reaches Haul Varder's feet, it begins spilling into the crevice, where it or the lava cease to exist.

At the same time, the tunnels on the far side grow brighter. The brightness emerges in globes of purest radiance. Some are smaller than others, but all resemble instances of the sun's best light. They float in the air without apparent aim, riding the breezes. Some are carried upward and swept away, funneled into the night above the mountain. Others bob here and there, avoiding only the flow of darkness on the floor. Those that collide with Haul Varder's fire do not harm him. They are not harmed themselves.

Driven by fear and eagerness, the hierophant retreats to the wall of the cavern. There he watches to see what his creation will do. He has no need or desire to control Varder. He has written his own protection into the man's chest. Now he feels a student of power's desire to learn where his efforts will lead.

The wheelwright peers at the eerie manifestations. He stamps a foot into liquid dark. He swats at floating bright. Then he laughs like thunder. The sound of his mirth and scorn stuns Black's hearing. It shakes the organs in Black's chest.

"Is this how your King responds?" Haul Varder asks. His voice is sure triumph. "He is a fool! These forces are mindless. They have no purpose. They cannot harm me. They cannot stop me.

"When I reach him, I will hold his terror in my hands!"

Sought tastes fulfillment. The King's powers do not hurt his creation. They cannot.

Nevertheless Black smiles once more, a smile that would chill the heart of any man able to recognize it. "You are mistaken," he replies to Tamlin Marker's killer. "They do not need minds. They have mine."

The sound of Varder's laughter scours the cavern, but Black does not heed him. With sigils, glyphs, and scarifications, the King's Justice reclaims his longsword. For this sorcery, evaporation and distance are not obstacles. The remaining fragments of his shaping suffice. They enable him to recall his blade from the ether of its dispersion.

Cooled by the frigid touch of dark, he has strength enough to cut the rope that holds his left wrist. Made brittle by flowing cold, the bonds that secure his ankles part more easily. Though much of his soul and his vitality are gone, he is able to stand.

Under his breath, he prays, "One last effort, my lord. With your help." Then he moves toward the wheelwright.

In a staggering run so that Sought's creation of fire and stone will not have time to slap him aside, he thrusts the length of his sword deep into Haul Varder's belly.

While the transformed man roars heat and fury, Black collapses to his knees. But he does not release his grip on his longsword.

Too late, Varder reaches for Black. He means to fling his foe into the fissure. He means to pluck the blade from his belly and shatter it. He is strong enough to crumple the finest steel, and his wound is no more than an annoyance. But before he can strike, dark flows up Black's body and arms, and a globe of bright bursts in the wheelwright's face. Dark secures Black's hands to the sword's hilt. The utter cold of dark follows Black's longsword into Haul Varder's vitals. And bright enters Varder's throat when he tries to roar. A light that lava cannot consume is agony in the wheelwright's gullet, the man's chest.

Stricken by more pain than his made flesh can endure, Varder topples backward. He falls into the fire and fury of his shaping, and does not rise again.

Black does not hear the old man's wail of frustration and terror as Sought flees from the cavern. Kneeling near the lip of the rift, Black smiles for the last time. But this smile threatens no one. It is glad and grateful, and it is all that he has left.

When he falls himself, slumping into the embrace of dark and bright beside the fissure, he is not afraid.

꙳

He does not know that time passes. He does not know how long he is unconscious. Yet by small increments he becomes aware that he is at peace. He has no fears and is not driven. For this he feels gratitude. He does not question it.

Eventually, however, his pain returns. Blunted at first, then more sharply, jagged distress reclaims the back of his skull. He has been maimed of several of his inlays, some of his scarifications have been damaged, and one or more of his glyphs and sigils have been ruined. His right arm tells him that it has been wrenched in its socket. Also he has many bruises. If his soul is at peace, his body is not. Each beat of his heart forces him to acknowledge that he is alive.

His hurts are a form of grief. He feels dampness on his cheeks and knows that he weeps.

Later he finds that he cannot imagine where he is. He lies on softness, is covered by softness. There are pressures around his head and body that suggest his wounds have been bound. But there was no softness in the cavern where Haul Varder suffered and died. There was no one alive to bandage Black's wounds.

Someone has cared for him.

The King? he wonders vaguely. In some way that Black cannot identify, he has been healed. Not made whole, precisely, but more whole than he was. The King is capable of such consideration. Yet Black knows of no sorcery that can transport him from the edge of death in the mountain to a place of comfort. He knows of no shaper who can apply bandages at any distance. And his pains assure him that his wounds have only been tended. They are not mended. If he has been healed, it is not a healing of his body.

When more time has passed, Black becomes aware that he is not alone. He hears the low murmur of voices. He hears a woman's muffled weeping, and a man's awkward attempts to soothe her. He feels a hovering presence.

Sighing because he has not been granted death, Black opens his eyes.

As his sight clears, he sees that he is lying in a bed in a small room. The bed and the room are those in which he parted from Jon Marker.

A man sits in a chair at the head of the bed. It is his presence that hovers. With an effort, Black recognizes Father Tenderson. The priest of Dark Enduring has finally summoned the courage to approach Jon Marker.

Against the wall where Black can see her when he turns his head, a woman sits with a child cradled in her lap. The woman is Rose, and she is weeping softly, restraining her sorrow as much as she can so that she will not disturb Black. The girl in her lap is her daughter, Arbor. Arbor is wrapped around herself, as rigid as death. A feverish sweat beads on her brow. Her eyes do not open. She does not appear to breathe. Her skin has the stricken hue of tallow. Her mother's caresses give her no solace.

Jon Marker stands beside Rose. His good face is twisted in distress, and he wrestles with himself to find words that will comfort Rose, though no one has comforted him. He knows her distress well.

Father Tenderson sees that Black's eyes are open. The tall priest leans closer. "Ah," he begins uncertainly. "Black. Sir. You are awake. Do not try to speak. Conserve your strength.

"You will wonder how you come to be here. There is much I do not know, but I will tell you what I can."

The sight of Arbor in Rose's arms tightens like a fist around Black's heart. He finds that some purposes do not end. They are like roads without destinations, or roads where every step is a destination. He twitches a hand to silence the priest. He does not need to hear Father Tenderson. Instead he coughs to clear his throat, though pain claws his chest as he does so. He fights a rawness that reaches from his mouth to his lowest belly until he is able to whisper, "No."

Father Tenderson leans still closer. "No? Sir? No?"

"The girl." Black coughs again, tearing scabbed wounds. "Arbor. Did she touch me?"

The priest is startled. His eyes grow wide. "She did. How do you know?"

Black shakes his head, dismissing questions and explanations. "Then help her."

He is too weak to do what must be done.

Abrupt tears come to the tall man's eyes. "Do you think I would not, if I could? She is beyond me. Touching you hurt her. I cannot account for it. She is beyond any healer."

Black aches for the strength to swear. "Stop," he croaks. "Forget yourself. Hear me.

"Your god does not answer prayer. The King does." Trembling, he thrusts away the blanket that covers him. "Touch me here." He shows Father Tenderson the three places on his body that compel the King's notice. "Hold your hands here. Speak in your heart of what the child has done. You will be heard."

The priest stares. Black's demand, and the sight of Black's shaping, shakes his courage to its poor foundations. There is a wildness in his stare. He considers himself a coward despite his self-justifications. If Rose had not asked him to introduce her to Jon Marker, and if she had not accompanied him to this bereft house, he would not have come. He would not sit at Black's side now.

But he is also ashamed of his weak spirit. He is ashamed of his hesitation. Arbor's plight is a blade twisting in his heart. Also he knows that in his place Father Whorry would act first and question the meaning of his deeds later.

Trembling himself, Father Tenderson rests his hands where Black has shown him. He does his best to forget that he is afraid. In silence, he describes what Arbor has done, and how she has been afflicted. As he does this, he feels a rush of weakness. He almost faints. He hears no answer.

Yet the room is suddenly crowded with light. An unspeakable cold fills the air.

An instant later, both light and cold are gone. Father Tenderson's weakness passes. He does not understand what has transpired. He has imagined—

But he sees Black relaxing. After a moment, he is sure that Black now breathes more easily. Black's faith is stronger than the priest's.

When Rose gasps, the suddenness of her outburst snatches Father Tenderson to his feet. Unnoticed, his chair clatters on the floor behind him. When he turns to Rose, he sees her arms wrapped around her daughter, and Arbor's arms clutching her mother's neck. Clinging to each other, both mother and daughter sob aloud. Now, however, their cries are relief and gladness. Arbor has returned from the horror of what she has done for Black.

Beside Rose and Arbor, Jon Marker kneels. He is unaware of himself as he closes his arms around them both. He shares their surprised joy. He needs it as much as they do.

After a few moments, the Dark priest retrieves his chair. He seats himself near Black again. He is still trembling, but now he trembles for different reasons.

He does not ask Black what has just happened. He has witnessed a mystery and will not question it. He has believed that men and women need to share what is in their hearts. Now he has seen his conviction confirmed. He calls it worship.

He cannot find words to express his appreciation. Also he suspects that Black has no use for it. "If you wish it," he says instead, "I will tell you now how you come to be here. I have no other gift to give."

When Black has considered his circumstances, and his desire for an end to his journeys, he manages a slight nod. Though his concern for Arbor is eased, he remains confounded. Why is he not dead? Why has he not been allowed to pass away? Whispering again, he admits his curiosity.

Father Tenderson replies with a smile that mixes rue and

wonder. "Much," he begins more briskly, "I cannot explain. I do not know what you have done. I do not know how you have survived it. Still a cloud has been lifted from my heart, and perhaps also from Settle's Crossways. Some questions I can answer.

"That you are here is Blossom's doing. To account for herself, she said only that she knew you were in danger. When her caravan left for the east, she halted in the place where she had last seen the hierophant Sought and his guards. With two of her men, she left the train and entered the forest to search for you. She did not know where you had gone, but she guessed that Sought's purpose, and yours, would take you to the mountain.

"Her guess was confirmed when she discovered Sought's corpse on the mountainside. She could not determine the cause of his death, though by appearance he died many days ago. Yet"—the priest takes a deep breath, holds it to steady himself, then releases it slowly—"he was neither decayed nor eaten. Rather he was clad in a thick hoarfrost despite the preceding night's warmth. Perhaps the cold preserved him. Certainly it preserved his last expression. He died with astonishment on his face."

As the servant of Dark Enduring speaks, Jon Marker rises to join him. Tamlin's father knows Kelvera's account. It was to him that she gave it. But he has embraced Rose and Arbor, and has found solace. Now he feels a need to gaze upon Black.

"Knowing then," continues Father Tenderson, "that she had guessed correctly, Blossom pursued her search. And after a time, she found you. You were being dragged among the trees by a horse. With what must have been your last strength, you had hooked your arm through one stirrup. By that means, the horse was able to pull you toward Settle's Crossways.

"Confident that the horse was yours, obedient to your bidding, she and her men lifted you onto their own mounts and followed the horse to this house. She could not explain the horse's choice, or yours. And she did not remain to hear what you would say when you awakened. If you awakened. When Jon Marker had helped you to his bed, she informed him that she was required by her caravan. Having told her tale, she and her men rode away."

Now Tamlin Marker's father speaks. He knows that he is in Black's debt, though he cannot explain the debt's terms. Certainly Black saved him from Ing Hardiston's ruffians, but his life is a small thing, and he places no great value on it. His sense of indebtedness is deeper. It is as the priest has said. A cloud has been lifted from his heart. He owes Black some acknowledgment.

"I was at my wit's end," he confesses. He speaks haltingly, unsure of what he must say. "I was able to bind your wounds. I settled you as comfortably as I could. But I did not know how to succor you. Did you need food or drink? I could not rouse you. Did you require a healer? I could not imagine a healer in Settle's Crossways who would know how to mend a man so cut and scarred and"—he falters until he finds a word—"and embellished from neck to foot. I floundered until Father Tenderson brought Rose and Arbor to aid me.

"And then—" His voice breaks. "Then I thought—"

The priest intervenes to spare Jon Marker. He has listened to the many woes and hurts and angers of Dark Enduring's worshippers. He has learned to keep his composure.

"By chance, however," he says, "or perhaps by some form of providence"—he smiles crookedly, knowing his role in his temple—"yesterday Rose asked me to introduce her and Arbor to Jon. In my timid fashion, I agreed to do so this morning. You know why I have not come before. We arrived to find this good man growing frantic.

"At once, however, other matters became more frightening than your straits. Seeing you, Arbor broke from her mother. 'He has holes in his soul!' she cried. 'He will die! I can heal them!'

"I was of no use. I did not understand. Nor did Jon. Before Rose could prevent her, Arbor ran to your side and placed her hands on your chest.

"At once, she screamed, a howl too fierce for so small a girl. Then she collapsed. She became the lost thing you saw in Rose's lap, a child overcome by who you are. By what you have done. By what was done to you. It was more than she could bear.

"We do not discount what you have endured. We will not. Still I say that her suffering was greater. You do not act in ignorance. You are able to estimate the cost of your deeds. She is not. She cannot prepare herself for the price of what she does.

"For that reason, I—" He glances around. "We?" When both Jon and Rose nod, he declares, "We will treasure what has been done for her above what has been done for us."

Black does not reply. He has no words. Indeed, he hardly attends to the priest. He approves Father Tenderson's sentiments. He wants no gratitude. To his way of thinking, he deserves none. He has merely served his purpose. But now a choice awaits him. He was not permitted to die. Therefore he is now free to determine how he will live. His wounds will heal. The remains of his shaping will suffice to mend him. And when he is well, what then?

He can attempt to make a home for himself in Settle's Crossways, or perhaps in some nearby town that is ignorant of him. He can join a caravan and accompany it wherever it goes. Or he can return to the King, where he will be shaped anew and dispatched to resume his purpose.

While Black searches himself, Father Tenderson and Rose agree to depart. The priest has his temple's duties, and Rose does not wish to tempt Arbor with Black's nearness. The mother promises Jon Marker that she will return later with food and better bandages. She smiles easily at his embarrassed thanks. Then she and Arbor are gone.

While Father Tenderson speaks briefly with Jon, Black rouses himself to forestall the priest's departure. The priest is as ignorant as Rose of Arbor's gifts. They will need a measure of guidance.

"Father," he says hoarsely. "Hear me a moment longer. I cannot explain Arbor's gifts. She will need her mother's protection, and yours." He has not strength enough to name Father Whorry also. "But when she is well again, she will be able to heal you. No harm will come to her."

Nor will she be harmed by giving her gift to Jon Marker, a man whom she will not be able to resist.

The priest is surprised. His head jerks up. His eyes grow wide. Is he in need of healing? Truly in need? He knows that he is, for the weakness in his soul when he touched Black, and for the weakness of his courage. But he does not know how he has become transparent to Black's discernment.

Another mystery. This one also he will not question. Instead he makes what he will later call a leap of faith. Bowing to Black, he says, "You have done enough. Settle's Crossways no longer needs the King's Justice."

He feels that he is fleeing as he leaves the room, the house. He wants time to think. More than that, he wants to consult with Father Whorry. He needs to hear his friend's simpler judgments of what he has seen and learned.

Alone, Jon Marker remains at Black's bedside. The wounded stranger's plight still perplexes his kindness, though he has been relieved by Black's awakening, and by Arbor's recovery, by Rose's generosity, and by the priest's easy spate of talk. He has not repaid his debt. He shifts from foot to foot. Stilted in his courtesy, he asks if Black needs water. He asks if Black can eat. He offers to make soup when he has fired the stove.

Black has no reply. His thoughts go elsewhere. As he regards his host, he considers his purpose in a new light. It is not an unending struggle against such men as Sought and Haul Varder. It is not measured by his opposition to bullies like Ing Hardiston. It stands at his bedside now. It belongs to men like the priests, to women like Rose, to children like Arbor and lost Tamlin.

When he is well, he will return to the King. He needs his purpose as much as it needs him.